'Two years ... **car crash,'** ...

'We were on ou... them about the ... Polly knew he'd ... her involuntary gasp but she hadn't been able to help it when she'd realised that he'd lost a baby too. . .

'What?' he demanded.

'Nothing,' she began. 'It's just that. . .' At the last moment, she stopped. She just couldn't face exposing her own pain. . .

Josie Metcalfe lives in Cornwall now with her long-suffering husband, four children and two horses, but, as an army brat frequently on the move, books became the only friends who came with her wherever she went. Now that she writes them herself she is making new friends, and hates saying goodbye at the end of a book—but there are always more characters in her head clamouring for attention until she can't wait to tell their stories.

Recent titles by the same author:

HEART SURGEON
VALENTINE'S HUSBAND
A WISH FOR CHRISTMAS
FOR NOW, FOR ALWAYS
WORTH WAITING FOR

FIRST THINGS FIRST

BY
JOSIE METCALFE

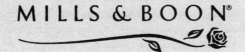

MILLS & BOON®

DID YOU PURCHASE THIS BOOK WITHOUT A COVER?
If you did, you should be aware it is **stolen property** as it was
reported *unsold and destroyed* by a retailer. Neither the Author
nor the publisher has received any payment for this book.

*All the characters in this book have no existence outside the imagina-
tion of the author, and have no relation whatsoever to anyone bearing
the same name or names. They are not even distantly inspired by any
individual known or unknown to the author, and all the incidents are
pure invention.*

*All Rights Reserved including the right of reproduction in whole or
in part in any form. This edition is published by arrangement with
Harlequin Enterprises II B.V. The text of this publication or any part
thereof may not be reproduced or transmitted in any form or by any
means, electronic or mechanical, including photocopying, recording,
storage in an information retrieval system, or otherwise, without the
written permission of the publisher.*

*This book is sold subject to the condition that it shall not, by way of
trade or otherwise, be lent, resold, hired out or otherwise circulated
without the prior consent of the publisher in any form of binding or
cover other than that in which it is published and without a similar
condition including this condition being imposed on the subsequent
purchaser.*

*MILLS & BOON and MILLS & BOON with the Rose Device
are registered trademarks of the publisher.*

*First published in Great Britain 1997
Harlequin Mills & Boon Limited,
Eton House, 18-24 Paradise Road, Richmond, Surrey TW9 1SR*

© Josie Metcalfe 1997

ISBN 0 263 80433 X

*Set in Times 10 on 11½ pt. by
Rowland Phototypesetting Limited
Bury St Edmunds, Suffolk*

03-9710-48330-D

*Printed and bound in Great Britain
by Mackays of Chatham PLC, Chatham*

CHAPTER ONE

HE SAT up in the pre-dawn chill and swung his legs over the side of the bed, bracing his elbows on his naked thighs. His shoulders slumped, his head dropping forward into his hands as his long fingers speared tiredly through the thick blond strands to massage the tension in his aching neck.

'So tired. . .' His deep voice was a husky rasp in the echoing darkness of the spartan room. 'So damn tired. . .'

Was he ever going to be able to sleep soundly again?

Would he ever be able to forget the events of that night, one year, eleven months and three weeks ago?

Forget. . .? Across the darkness of the room his eyes sought the pale shape, not needing to see the photograph clearly to know what it represented.

How could he forget when he had survived and she. . .*they* had died?

It was *that* guilt which wouldn't let him rest; which returned to torment him each time he closed his eyes and tried to lose himself in the oblivion of sleep.

In the meantime, all he could do was fill every waking hour with work and more work—anything to keep his brain occupied; anything to stop him dreading what would happen when he came home and tried to sleep.

'Well, *he's* certainly no Prince Charming!' somebody muttered into the uncomfortable silence after Nicholas Prince swept out of the room.

5

Polly knew she shouldn't but, in spite of her burning cheeks, she couldn't help herself from joining in the quiet gust of laughter which swept the scattering of people gathered in the small staffroom. At least it broke the tension which the irate consultant had left behind him.

Unfortunately, she thought as she turned to go back to work, such scenes had been happening more and more frequently over the last week. This latest episode had been the worst of the lot, and she wondered if it was time she spoke to someone about it.

It was a good sign that the rest of the staff could still crack a joke and laugh about the situation, but in the high-pressure world of St Augustine's Accident and Emergency Department it could be dangerous if one member of staff was endangering the working relationship of the team—especially such a senior member.

'Are you all right, Polly?' Hannah Nicholls demanded quietly. 'Old Nick's tongue can flay the skin off you at twenty paces.'

Polly had thought she'd been alone and had allowed her slender shoulders to droop, grateful for a few moments to regain her composure. Before Hannah had spoken she'd begun to check off the fresh stock needed to replenish the supplies they'd used in stabilising and patching up the first influx of accident victims on this rainy autumn Friday evening.

With a brief sigh she straightened determinedly as she turned to face her colleague with a smile of reassurance in her dark eyes.

'I'm fine, Hannah,' she said evenly and took the bull by the horns. 'Dr Prince had every right to criticise the state of readiness of the department and, in the absence of Sister MacDonald, it was my job to make sure that. . .'

'Rubbish!' Hannah interrupted loyally, the dark blue of her eyes almost spitting sparks as she leapt to Polly's defence. 'This place has been bedlam for the last hour. Oh, I grant you, there wasn't anything major, but it still wasn't reasonable for him to expect it to look like a showcase.'

'Except that the next batch of patients will expect the unit to be functioning at peak efficiency, and they'd be right,' Polly pointed out fairly, in spite of the fact that, inside, she was still burning with mortification.

'Even so, he had no right to take you to task in front of everyone like that,' Hannah complained, her short dark curls bouncing as she shook her head indignantly. 'He *knew* how busy you'd been with that elderly mugging victim going into shock.'

'It's all part of the job,' Polly returned calmly as she smoothed a stray wisp of her own shiny bob away from her eyes. She knew that if she so much as hinted that she agreed with Hannah it could only make a bad situation worse. The last thing the department needed in the existing uneasy atmosphere was for people to take sides in an unofficial war, no matter how much she'd like to tell Prince Charming what she thought of him. . .

'Well, *I* think you ought to tell him that you won't stand for it. . .' she began heatedly.

For the first time in a long time Polly actually blessed the interruption of the telephone as Hannah was forced to subside in mid-flow. She appreciated her friend's unstinting support, but just at the moment. . .

'A and E,' she said, and raised a hand to still Hannah in her tracks, then beckoned her back when she heard the hurried message. 'When can we expect them to arrive?' she demanded as she glanced down at the watch pinned to the front of her dark blue uniform, then pulled a face when the voice on the other end embarked on a lengthy explanation.

'Can you patch me through?' she interrupted. 'One of the paramedics could give me an update. . .' She covered the mouthpiece to speak rapidly to Hannah. 'Tell Dr Prince we've got another lot coming in across country. Multiple pile-up. ETA ten minutes. They're connecting me up with the emergency units so I can find out more details, but if you could let him know so he can decide whether to authorise a call-in for extra staff. . .'

Her attention was drawn back to the phone again, her hand automatically reaching for the pen in her top pocket as the information began pouring down the line. Out of the corner of her eye she saw the newly installed computer link chatter into activity as it began to display the vital signs of the first badly injured patient in transit.

'What have you got?' a husky baritone demanded abruptly from a point just behind her left ear. Polly glanced towards the familiar sound, and when she found his tall figure looming over her sidestepped to allow him to read her notes as she reached out to replace the phone.

'Multiple pile-up almost exactly halfway between here and St Mary's,' she clarified, mentioning the much smaller hospital to the north of St Augustine's. 'Obviously they're not equipped to deal with anything this big. . .'

'So they're dumping them onto us,' he finished for her, tight-lipped, his grey eyes as cold as winter.

'Of course,' she agreed, outwardly calm in spite of the way she had begun to seethe inside. He knew as well as she did that it was policy to send all the victims to the same hospital—the nearest one equipped to handle a large influx of injuries. 'We're newer and better equipped, while St Mary's isn't much bigger than a cottage hospital. They certainly haven't got the intensive care facilities that we have or the staff to call on.'

For a second there was silence, almost as if her sharp reply had surprised him. She could feel him radiating disapproval, but she didn't dare look up at him and kept her eyes fixed on the series of forms she was lining up.

'Well, I hope we can put up a more polished show than we did earlier on or, inadequate as it is, they'd be better off at St Mary's,' he finally growled as he responded to the approaching sound of sirens and turned to stride away.

Robbed of speech by his abrupt rudeness, she stared daggers at the breadth of his departing back, only managing to mutter a deep-felt, 'Bloody man,' before she was inundated with people demanding her attention.

Polly led her team of nurses into action with practised ease, pleased with their smooth efficiency.

As each ambulance disgorged its load of victims the current status of their injuries was checked against the paramedics' reports and they were swiftly dispersed.

In the case of the more seriously wounded, the advance information they'd received over the computer link meant that they could be sent immediately up to a theatre which was ready and waiting for their arrival.

The less seriously injured disappeared straight into one or other of the designated treatment rooms for attention, while those who had been lucky enough to have received more minor injuries were directed to seats in the reception area to wait patiently for attention.

'There are so many of them,' Hannah muttered in an

aside to Polly as their paths crossed yet again as they
dodged through a mêlée of junior doctors and extra
nursing staff, ending up entering the same treatment
room together. 'Does anyone know what happened?'
she asked under the all too familiar hubbub of questions
and orders, all overlaid by the wails and groans of
injured humanity.

'Apparently, the brakes failed on a coach as it was
coming down a steep hill towards a junction, and it
ploughed into the back of a second coach waiting at
traffic lights,' Polly replied.

'Well, why are there so many hip and knee injuries?'
Tina Wadland questioned, still slightly overawed by her
first day in A and E as she finished cutting a pair of
jeans off a patient. The paramedics had already split
them up to mid-thigh at the scene of the crash to enable
them to tape a dressing over the patient's badly lacerated
knee, but now she had the task of removing the rest of
his clothing.

'At a guess, that's because when one coach hit the
other, it pushed the rows of seats forward so the passen-
gers' legs were trapped against the seats in front,' Polly
hazarded as she and the waiting porter loaded her patient
and his newly developed X-rays for transfer up to
Orthopaedics and the start of a lengthy acquaintanceship
with a bulky plaster cast.

Still, she thought as she stripped off her gloves and
disposed of them, from the discussion she'd overheard
in front of the X-ray viewbox between Nicholas Prince
and the orthopaedic consultant, Alex Marshall, the
coach driver had been lucky to escape a trip to Theatre
for the surgical realignment of his broken bones.

'You'll probably find that there are quite a few whip-
lash injuries, too,' she continued in a quiet aside to

Tina as she snapped a fresh pair of gloves in position. 'Especially the people who didn't have their heads resting back against the seat at the time of impact, or didn't have time to brace themselves.'

A swift glance up at the clock told her that she should have gone off duty nearly an hour ago, but she mentally shrugged her resignation as she reached for the next set of forms and departed to collect her next patient, momentarily feeling rather as if she were working on a factory production line.

For a second she stood to one side of the waiting area and cast her eyes over the remaining group of people and belongings. As she mentally thanked whatever stroke of luck had enabled the majority of the patients to escape serious injury, one hand surreptitiously massaged the tight muscles in the small of her back before she drew in a deep breath and prepared to enter the fray once more.

'Standing and looking at the job doesn't get it done, Sister Lang,' growled a harsh voice. 'Every second you spend standing idly by means that someone else has to work harder and longer.'

Without so much as a glance in his direction, she knew whose acid words they were and her shoulders stiffened defensively before she could hide her reaction, her shock at the unwarranted attack drawing her eyes up to clash with the turbulent grey of Nicholas Prince's angry gaze.

'Well?' he prompted in an abrupt undertone. 'Are you waiting for a personal invitation to treat another patient? In which case, consider yourself invited. There are several people still waiting for lacerations to be stitched, and the longer they're left the less chance there is of making a good job of it.'

Overriding the stab of hurt at the injustice of his attack, Polly was suddenly struck by the awful desire to salute him as if he were some despotic sergeant major. Luckily, before she had a chance to follow through he was striding across the room towards his beckoning registrar, and she buried the insane urge under another hour of frantic activity.

'Well, in spite of what Old Nick says, I reckon we did well with that little lot,' Hannah mumbled round a mouthful of sandwich as she watched Polly gather up her belongings. 'Mind you, I don't think we'd have managed quite so well if you hadn't stayed on to help out.'

'Rubbish,' Polly muttered, bending forward to change her shoes in an attempt to hide the rising colour in her cheeks. 'There were quite a few people who responded to the call-in. I'm only another pair of hands.'

'Only another pair of hands? Hah!' scoffed her friend. 'You're only the best qualified member of nursing staff in the department, and that includes Big Mac,' she added, irreverently referring to Senior Sister Celia MacDonald. '*And* you were the most senior one here this evening who was in at the beginning of Old Nick's reorganisation. You'd think he'd be more appreciative.'

Polly clenched her teeth. She wasn't going to touch *that* topic with a bargepole.

'Why do you call him Old Nick?' she demanded in a rather blatant attempt at sidetracking Hannah. 'He might have the start of grey hair among the blond, but he's not that much older than we are—what is he, mid to late thirties?'

'It's got nothing to do with his age, although he certainly acts as bad-tempered as if he were middle-aged,' Hannah replied with a scowl. 'It's more to do with the fact that he breathes fire and brimstone like the devil himself—you ought to know about that. You've been in the firing line several times today.'

Since she'd first started her hospital training Polly had made a point of largely ignoring the gossip passed around on the hospital grapevine, and was going to let the comment pass unremarked as she straightened up with her bag in her hand—only to find herself tempted to probe.

'Hannah. . . God knows he's always been a bit of a perfectionist, but this is something else. Something. . .' She shrugged, at a loss for words. 'Have *you* any idea what's been setting him off the last couple of days?'

'You mean, apart from you?' Hannah gibed wryly.

'Seriously,' Polly said with a grimace. 'I know he's had a lot on his plate in the last year with the reorganisation of the department, and we know from the moans and groans that it's meant a return to shiftwork for the consultants to provide the twenty-four-hour supervisory cover. . .' She paused briefly to organise her thoughts.

'I thought the new rota had been in operation long enough for most of the kinks to be ironed out and lift the pressure off him a bit, but he seems. . .exhausted,' she finished with a shrug.

'You're right on all counts,' Hannah agreed as she folded the empty sandwich wrapper into an aeroplane and aimed it successfully at the bin, before glancing up at Polly. 'In theory, the new system should be spreading the load but lately it seems as if the daft man doesn't know when to stop. For example, today he was supposed to go home when Leo came on duty.'

'You mean he's been here for. . .' she paused for some mental arithmetic '. . .eighteen hours?'

'At least—especially if he turned up early this

morning,' Hannah confirmed. 'It makes you wonder if he's got a home to go to.'

Polly had enough to think about without speculating as to Nicholas Prince's living arrangements, and she wished Hannah a quiet end to her shift before she made a quick detour into the staff cloakroom.

Polly wasn't aware of having opened the door particularly quietly, but the only other occupant of the hushed surroundings must have been totally unaware that she had company as she continued to weep with quiet intensity.

'Tina?' Polly said softly, as she abandoned her bags on the corner of the vanity shelf surrounding the hand-basins and wrapped a consoling arm around the shuddering shoulders. 'What's the matter? Is it anything I can help with?'

'Oh, Sister!' she wailed, trying to stifle the sound with a large handful of tissues. 'It's no use. . .*I'm* no use! I'll *never* get it right!'

'Get what right?' Polly prompted as she grabbed a couple of paper towels from the dispenser and wet them under the cold tap, before offering them to Tina to cool her blotchy face.

Polly soon pieced together Tina's tale of woe and her anger rose again when she realised that once more Dr Nicholas Prince was the cause of the upset.

'Don't let it get you down, Tina,' she advised while the youngster blew her nose and tidied herself. 'We were all new to the department once. You'll learn soon enough.'

Polly was proud of the calm way she was able to deliver the encouraging speech, knowing that her inner anger was hidden behind her smile as she sent the young nurse back to work. It was a different matter when the door swung shut and she was alone in the cloakroom, and it was several minutes before she felt sufficiently composed to go out and look for the consultant.

'Enough is enough,' she muttered belligerently as she retrieved her bags and elbowed her way out into the corridor. 'It's time someone told him where to get off. . . Ah! Leo!' she called, catching sight of the registrar just as he was disappearing round a corner, and his head reappeared briefly.

'Hello, Polly, my love. I thought you'd gone home,' he said with his trademark killer smile as he approached her, his hair gleaming gold under the bright lights of the corridor. 'Can't stay away from me, eh? I knew you'd fall for my charms if I waited long enough!'

'In your dreams!' Polly retorted, the answering smile drawn out of her by his usual light-hearted nonsense.

'You wound me, heartless wench,' he complained, covering his heart dramatically with both hands. 'Your scorn will send me home tonight to weep into my pillow.'

'Hah!' she scoffed, but his teasing words had reminded her of the reason she'd called him. 'Speaking of crying,' she began determinedly, all trace of humour wiped from her face, 'can you tell me where your boss is hiding? I need to have a word with him.'

'Anything I can help with?' Leo offered, the levity gone from his voice, too, with the return of his professional persona.

'Not this time,' she said briefly, deliberately witholding an explanation. *This* was something which she needed to do face to face.

'I see,' Leo said thoughtfully, his tawny gaze scanning her face with quiet intensity before she caught a strange hint of approval. 'Only Nick will do?'

Polly was very conscious of his assessing look and nearly protested his choice of words, but in essence Leo was right. Dr Prince's behaviour over the last couple of days was becoming unacceptable and, while anyone could be excused for having a bad day, he was rapidly approaching the point where he could be reported to the 'three wise men' for a warning of disciplinary action.

'It's important that I speak with him personally,' she agreed, only her conviction that she was doing the right thing keeping her voice even.

'In that case. . .' Leo fished through an overladen pocket and pulled out a notepad, emblazoned with a drugs company logo. 'Here.' He held out a swiftly scribbled note. 'He went home about fifteen minutes ago, but that's the address.'

'Oh, but. . .' Polly was taken aback. It was one thing to confront the A and E consultant about a problem at work, but another thing entirely to carry the complaint to his own home.

'It's only a stone's throw away. . .unless you'd rather I dealt with it?'

There was a strange tone to Leo's voice, almost as if he was taunting her—or daring her to carry through with her intention.

'Thank you for the offer, but it won't be necesssary,' Polly said with a glance at the hieroglyphic scrawl and a conscious lift of her chin. 'I have to go in that direction on my way home. I'm sure I'll be able to find him.'

'I'm sure you shall,' Leo murmured blandly as she turned away, and she was conscious that he watched her retreating back all the way to the next corner in the corridor.

A squadron of butterflies had begun to hatch out inside her and were warming up for a spectacular aerobatic display by the time she'd walked half way to her destination, and it was only the memory of Tina's tearful face that stiffened her resolve.

If Nicholas Prince's venom had only been directed towards herself it wouldn't have mattered so much—she was an experienced nurse who'd learned to put up with the abuse hurled at her from the less amiable sections of society, and her own personal life had taught her how to turn the other cheek.

'But when he starts in on a newcomer as green as Tina it's time someone told him the facts of life.'

Her pulse rate skipped as she realised the temerity of her actions. It was all too possible that she might be making a big mistake; might even make a bad situation worse, but. . .

'Here we go,' she muttered as she paused in the gathering dusk to peer at the number Leo had written down for her, and climbed the shallow steps of the solid Georgian house.

The sound of the chimes had long faded away into the depths of the house and she shivered in the autumn chill as she impatiently pressed the button a second time. Almost immediately light streamed out into the encroaching darkness from the fanlight window over the heavy panelled wooden door.

'All right, all right, I'm coming,' growled a deep voice, as she heard the sound of heavy bolts being drawn.

'Ah, the familiar dulcet tones,' she whispered to herself in an attempt at stiffening her suddenly shaky resolve.

The door swung open and she was almost blinded by the sudden flood of light, her nemesis appearing as a large black silhouette as he stepped into the bright opening.

'What the. . .? Sister Lang?' Surprise robbed his voice of bite. 'What are you. . .? Do you need to see me? What's the matter? Has something gone wrong since I left? Is my pager on the blink?' He fired the questions at her one after the other, without allowing her time to think—let alone answer.

'Yes. . . No. . .I mean, as far as I know, there's nothing wrong with your pager, but I do need to see you.' She was almost squinting up at him as the light poured into her face, trying vainly to decipher his hidden expression.

There were several seconds of silence before he stepped back from the doorway and, pulling the door wide, gestured for her to enter.

As the door swung shut behind her she turned to face him, and suddenly realised that he was less than fully dressed. As her eyes were filled with the unexpected sight of his naked chest a flood of embarrassment heated her cheeks.

'I'm sorry, I didn't realise that you were getting ready for b-bed. Perhaps I'd better speak to you tomorrow. . .' She inwardly cursed the juvenile stammer as she turned back towards the door and reached up to release the catch.

'No.' A lean-fingered hand covered hers briefly and she froze, the electricity of the light contact preventing her from turning the knob as effectively as if he'd used brute force, before he snatched it away and continued speaking. 'If your mission was important enough to have you tracking me down then I'd better find out what it's all about, hadn't I? Can I offer you a drink?'

His voice receded and she turned towards him, her

eyes reluctantly following his silent steps as he walked
away from her down the empty hallway.

'But. . .'

She realised that there was no point in objecting to
his high-handedness when he continued to stride away
from her through an open doorway and disappeared
from view, completely ignoring her attempt at speech.

'Coffee?' he prompted when she hesitantly followed
him into the stark newness of a recently refurbished
kitchen. 'Or can I offer you something stronger if you're
off duty for the day. . .?' He reached for the solitary
glass residing on the otherwise pristine work-surface
and toasted her with the inch and a half of amber-
coloured liquid in the bottom.

'No. Thank you for the offer but. . .' She felt quite
uncomfortable with the thought of accepting a drink
from him when she had come to tell him what she
thought of his rotten temper.

'Oh, for heaven's sake!' He slapped the glass down
but hardly seemed to notice that the contents splashed
up the sides and over his hand. 'It would hardly consti-
tute a gross impropriety if you were to accept a drink
from me. What do you think I'm going to do—publicise
the fact on a noticeboard? Everyone in A and E already
knows you well enough to realise there'd be nothing
personal in your acceptance!'

Polly was shocked into silence, her feelings of hurt
at the unexpected attack widening her eyes as she stared
at him, but even so she was still aware of a deep under-
lying bitterness in his voice.

Before she had a chance to do any more than register
the twist of distaste which marred his face he swung
away from her, his fingers spearing through the thick
blond strands of his hair as he sighed heavily and

dropped his head forward to massage the back of his neck.

'God, I'm sorry,' he said, rubbing both hands roughly over his face as he turned to face her again. 'That was totally uncalled-for.'

Polly agreed silently, suddenly aware of just how tired he looked. If it had only been the result of a self-inflicted long day's work she could have understood it, but this was something more—this was something bone-deep and it looked as if he wasn't coping with it.

'I'd better go,' Polly murmured, uncomfortably aware of the fact that his vulnerability was pulling at her, persuading her to drop her own animosity towards him. 'I can speak to you when you come on duty tomorrow.'

She turned to leave the kitchen.

'*If* I go on duty. . .'

She almost missed the words he murmured under his breath, but something make her turn back in time to see the flash of empty desolation in his eyes.

'I thought you were on early tomorrow?' she queried, and saw the way the corners of his mouth tightened before he turned away from her gaze to pick up his glass again.

'Yes,' he confirmed with a weary sigh, and flung the remaining liquid to the back of his throat with a well-practised flick of his wrist. The half-melted ice cubes hardly had time to settle in the bottom of the glass before he was reaching for the bottle. 'Are you sure I can't offer you one for the road? It's supposed to help you sleep.' He raised a questioning eyebrow and waved the bottle at her before he twisted the cap off and poured a generous amount over the tinkling ice.

Something in his tone made Polly pause before she spoke, her eyes running over him more analytically than before.

This time, instead of shying away from the fact that the all-too-attractive A and E consultant in front of her was clad only in a pair of hip-hugging jeans with his broad naked chest on view, she made herself take note of the fact that he didn't look as if he weighed as much as he should.

In fact, now that she thought about it, he seemed to have lost quite a bit of weight over the last couple of weeks, his face having take on a lean, fine-drawn edge, with hollows under his cheek-bones and shadows under his enigmatic eyes.

More convinced than ever that his sour temper around the department had a serious cause, and her heart softening irrevocably towards him, she finally took her courage in both hands.

'Do you have any "unleaded" coffee?' she asked as casually as she could manage, and had the pleasure of seeing that she had stopped him in his tracks, his lean hand holding the glass suspended in mid-air on its way to his mouth.

'I don't know,' he said, obviously bemused as he turned back towards her. 'Do you want me to look?'

'Either that, or tea,' she confirmed with a tentative smile. 'I find that ordinary coffee keeps me awake if I drink it too late in the evening.' She eyed the newly filled glass in his hand and chanced an explosion. 'Will you be joining me?'

There was a pause while his gaze homed in sharply on her face and then, just as she felt the heat beginning to rise in her cheeks, one corner of his mouth lifted in a wry grin.

'It wasn't subtle, but you made your point,' he said gruffly as he reached out his hand and tipped the contents of the glass into the sink, the ice-cubes clattering loudly as they landed on the stainless steel. He slid the bottle to the back corner of the work surface and turned towards the kettle. 'But, if I'm joining you, it will have to be a coffee. I can't make tea at this time of night. . .'

He paused, a strange expression crossing his face as he pressed his lips together in a grim line.

'Oh, God,' he muttered and closed his eyes as if in defeat.

'If it's a problem. . .' Polly began, not understanding the last few seconds at all. For a moment it had looked as if it was going to be all right, but suddenly. . .

'No. . . It's not a problem. At least. . .' He shook his head as he continued, the words emerging almost as if they were being dragged out of him. 'The smell of tea makes. . .made Dee feel sick so I stopped drinking it in the evening.'

'Dee?' Polly questioned faintly, shocked to feel a sharp twist of disappointment when she heard him say the woman's name.

'Deanne. . .' he elaborated. 'My wife.'

CHAPTER TWO

'YOUR wife?' Polly repeated in consternation, her eyes flicking around the pristine room for some sign of a woman's touch. 'I'm sorry, I didn't know. . . Leo didn't tell me that you're married or I'd never have disturbed you at home. . .at this time of night. . .'

She was scrambling for words to express her apologies, once more avoiding looking directly at the expanse of naked flesh Nicholas was displaying. Now that she knew he had a wife she felt even more awkward about being in the same room with him while he was wearing so little.

Had he been getting ready to go to bed with her? Had he had to pull some clothes on to cover his nakedness to answer the bell?

She started edging uncomfortably towards the door.

For the first time in several years she found herself fighting the mental image of a naked man and, what was worse, it was St Augustine's A and E consultant—and a married man—whose body she was imagining.

Her cheeks flamed as she studiously avoided looking at him and reached for the latch.

'I'm not,' he said abruptly, bringing her up short as her eyes darted up to meet his in confusion. 'Not any more,' he clarified, his voice a harsh rasp in the silence.

'Not?' Polly blinked, questions whirling around so fast inside her head that she couldn't catch hold of any of them for long enough to formulate them into an intelligible sentence, let alone dare to ask them.

Were he and his wife separated? Divorced?

'She died,' he said bluntly, as though that was the only way he could bring himself to say it. 'A year and. . .two years ago in a car crash.'

The words hovered in the air between them, the hollow sound of his voice seeming to echo endlessly inside her head.

'Oh, God, I'm sorry,' she said helplessly, her heart going out to him. She knew only too well how it felt to suffer such a devastating loss. 'I had no idea. . .'

'Very few people do.' His voice sounded rough, as though it still hurt to talk about it. 'I moved to St Augustine's after I. . .shortly after it happened so. . .' He shrugged dismissively. 'There was no need for anyone to know.'

Polly's mind was churning furiously now as she started to collect the snippets of information he was giving her, and the picture which she was building was beginning to sound very familiar.

'What time of year did it happen?' she asked, deciding on an oblique approach.

'Autumn,' he said, the slight frown indicating his puzzlement at the apparently random question, and when she remained silent he elaborated. 'The first weekend in October. We were on our way to visit her parents to tell them about the baby. . .' His voice trailed away. She knew he'd heard her involuntary gasp but she hadn't been able to help it when she'd realised that he'd lost a baby too. . .

'What?' he demanded.

'Nothing,' she began, but she could see from his expression that he wasn't going to believe her denial. 'It's just that. . .'

At the last moment she couldn't face exposing her

own pain and settled for voicing her second thought.

'It's almost *exactly* two years ago, isn't it?' she asked softly, knowing from her own experience that she could be touching open wounds.

'Tomorrow,' he admitted after an interminable pause, his eyes dark and empty. 'It will be two years tomorrow evening.'

'Oh, I'm so sorry,' she breathed as all her suspicions were confirmed, and she reached out to lay one gentle hand over his clenched fist in an involuntary expression of kinship. 'It's bad enough that it happened, but I know it's even harder when you get to the anniversaries. . .'

He stiffened in automatic rejection of her sympathetic touch, his eyes meeting hers in a stormy grey glare which denied pity. It was difficult but she bit her lip and managed to hold his gaze steadily, her own memories bringing the warning burn that tears weren't far away.

'You're not just taking pot-shots in the dark, are you?' he said finally, his voice sounding almost resigned as he recognised a fellow sufferer. 'How long has it been for you?'

'Nearly five years,' she confirmed. 'And, before you ask, no, it never goes away but, yes, it does eventually get easier to live with.'

There was little amusement in his brief laugh.

'Sometimes I think a lifetime won't be long enough,' he admitted in that awful hollow tone, and Polly felt a shiver travel up her spine as his words echoed inside her head.

Somewhere, in one of the rooms along the hallway, a clock chimed and the strangely uneasy silence was broken, but he spoke before Polly could find the words to make her excuses and go.

'I'm sorry, I still haven't made you that drink,' he

said apologetically as he reached out to switch on the kettle. 'By the way, why *did* you come after me this evening?'

Polly's heart sank. What could she say now that wouldn't seem like kicking a man when he was already down?

On the other hand, she argued silently, didn't she have a responsibility towards the younger members of staff—the ones who weren't in any position to remonstrate with an obstreperous consultant without making the complaint official?

'Ah!' Her silence had obviously gone on just too long and his intelligent brain was sifting unspoken information at lightning speed. 'In the absence of Sister MacDonald, were you nominated to beard the lion in his den? What is it that they want me to do—reorganise the duty roster or represent the department at one of those interminable fund-raising events? It's not something to do with the Autumn Ball?'

'No. . .not exactly,' Polly hedged while she cast about frantically for inspiration and came up empty-handed. 'It's not quite. . . It's rather. . . Oh, damn,' she muttered, wishing that she'd never had the bright idea of confronting him—and especially not this evening. Why hadn't she left it until next week?

After tomorrow night he would probably revert to being his usual serious, unflappable self and they'd all wonder what the fuss had been about—but, then, until a few minutes ago she hadn't known the reason why he'd been so. . .

'Spit it out,' he advised. 'Whatever it is, it's now considered illegal to kill the bearers of bad news so you're relatively safe.'

'Thanks!' She grimaced wryly as she clenched her

hands into fists inside the pockets of her down-filled jacket, feeling more uncomfortable with every passing minute. 'Except that it's not quite that easy to. . .'

'Oh, for heaven's sake!' he exploded, his meagre store of patience obviously exhausted. 'I know you haven't come here to proposition me and you've already told me I didn't leave any problems behind at St Augustine's so. . .'

'Actually, sir, that's not strictly true,' Polly broke in nervously, peripherally aware that she still wasn't certain what to call him in an off-duty situation, especially as her task was work-related.

'But when you arrived you told me that there wasn't a problem back at St Augustine's,' he objected harshly.

'That's not exactly. . .' she began, then froze when he took a swift step towards her, his six feet of lean masculine height making him loom almost menacingly over her much shorter five feet four.

'Then what *exactly* is it about?' He mimicked her choice of words cruelly. 'These days I haven't got a great deal of patience with people who won't come to the point.'

His words were just enough to stiffen her resolve, and her chin lifted belligerently as she glared at him out of dark brown eyes.

'Actually, *that's* what I came to see you about, sir,' she found herself announcing with barely a quiver in her voice. 'There have been several complaints from some of the younger nurses, as well as the other staff in the department, that lately you have been unnecessarily. . .' she hunted around frantically for an acceptable word '. . .harsh. . .with your criticisms.'

'Good God!' His astonishment sounded loud and clear. 'You mean to tell me you followed me home because some wet-behind-the-ears junior had a fit of the vapours when I told them off for falling down on the job?'

'Hardly,' she denied shortly. 'It was more a case of wanting to have a word with you to find out whether you had a valid reason for your unreasonable behaviour and,' she continued, determined to finish what she'd started in spite of his attempt at interruption, 'to warn you that if it went on much longer you were going to find yourself paying a visit to the "three wise men" in the near future.'

She thought it was her reference to the the hospital disciplinary committee which stopped him in his tracks because he'd looked ready to explode right up until she used their slightly tongue-in-cheek nickname.

There was nearly a minute of utter silence, except for the frantic beating of her heart which seemed to fill the room.

'Oh, hell,' he finally muttered as he dragged the fingers of both hands through his thick blond hair.

Polly released the breath she hadn't been aware of holding, her nerves still wound tight enough to send her into orbit when the kettle suddenly shrieked.

'Look, I won't stay for a drink now.' A late attack of cowardice had her hurrying into speech as she saw him turn to switch the noise off and open the honey-coloured wooden cupboard door to reach for two mugs. 'If you're on early tomorrow you'll want to go to sleep fairly soon. . .'

'Chance would be a fine thing,' he muttered bitterly as he braced his hands on the counter and hung his head forward, the broad nakedness of his shoulders rounding almost defensively. 'Please,' he murmured, his husky voice barely louder than a whisper, 'keep me company—just for the time it takes to drink a cup of coffee?'

Polly had the feeling that Dr Nicholas Prince didn't ask for favours easily and her heart melted.

She knew what it felt like to dread coming home to the lonely silence of an empty house; knew how hard it was to keep busy enough to stop your mind going over and over the same desperate series of events. She knew what it was like to lie awake, staring into the darkness and wishing that somehow you could go back in time and alter the course of your own personal history—to have the chance to change the single event that would switch it from tragedy back to happiness.

Wordlessly she pulled out a chair and sat at the table, one corner of her mind registering the simplicity of the design of the furniture and the soft patina of the freshly finished wood, while the rest of her senses were tuned to the man standing silently on the other side of the room.

When he didn't move she realised that he hadn't seen what she had done.

'A splash of milk and half a sugar,' she prompted and saw him stiffen with shock before he whirled towards her, disbelief clear on his face.

'What?' He was obviously bemused.

'In my coffee,' she elaborated patiently. 'I like it with a splash of milk and half a sugar, but don't make it too strong.'

He gazed at her a second longer before he turned away silently and reached up again for the two mugs.

While he was busy she gave herself permission to admire the smooth movement of the broad sheets of muscles across his back and the tension in his shoulder and arm as he lifted the kettle to pour water onto the spoonful of granules he'd deposited in each.

Without a word he carried both mugs over in one hand, juggling the sugar bowl, spoon and milk in the other as he deposited them on the table in front of her and pulled out a chair for himself on the other side.

After a quiet, 'Thanks,' Polly concentrated on adding the milk and sugar to her cup and stirred as if her life depended on it, all the while excruciatingly aware that they were separated by just the width of the table.

'Thank *you*.'

His husky voice drew her eyes up from their preoccupation with the ripples on the top of her coffee and she hesitantly met the pewter-coloured depths of his.

'What for?' she said, uncomfortably aware of the intensity of his gaze. '*You* provided the coffee.'

He shook his head.

'I don't know how but you know damn well that it wasn't just the cup of coffee,' he said with low vehemence and sipped at his own jet-black mugful.

Polly *did* know what he meant, and because her own heart still clenched in her chest at the memories she made herself voice some of her thoughts.

'It. . . It's the simple fact that someone else is in the house,' she said huskily, flicking a quick glance up at him and seeing his knuckles tighten around the mug as she continued softly, 'Someone else moving, making noise, breathing. . .'

His murmur of agreement was a low rumble in the depths of his chest and she watched him draw in a deep breath and release it slowly.

'Have I really been bad?' he asked quietly, all the fire gone.

'Awful,' Polly said. 'And the worst of it was the fact that none of us knew why and no one dared to ask.'

'And I can't even guarantee that the situation is going

to get any better,' he added despondently. 'God knows what I was like last year—no one said anything—so I don't know whether I'm still getting worse or gradually improving.'

'If this is an improvement I'm glad I didn't see you last time!' she dared, and was pleased to see the lightening of his expression, no matter how reluctant it was.

'All I've got to do now is get through tomorrow,' he said sombrely. 'It would be a crime to wish for back-to-back casualties, but I've seriously been thinking about sending the rest of the team home and doing twenty-four hours straight through myself.'

'Just like the good old days?' Polly questioned with a raised eyebrow. 'A and E staff risking serious misdiagnoses because they're dead on their feet?'

'God forbid! That's what the new regime is supposed to replace.'

'Well, then, there isn't a lot of sense in going back to it, is there?' she pointed out. 'Wouldn't it be better if you worked your assigned shift, then planned to do something else to occupy the rest of the day? Perhaps that way you won't get quite so tired and you won't be chewing pounds and spitting pennies. . .'

This time the chuckle came a little more easily and Polly was able to leave shortly afterwards with the memory of the husky sound still echoing in her ears.

'He might not have wished for it, but it looks as if he got it anyway,' Polly muttered to herself the next morning when it looked as if the A and E reception area was going to overflow. 'It looks as if the world and his wife are here.'

She held her hand out for the next batch of case

notes and followed the wheelchair through to the treatment room.

'Good morning, Mr Chandralal. I'm Sister Lang. What have you done to yourself?'

While the elderly man began to explain in great detail how he had come to stab a garden fork through his foot Polly helped him up onto the examination couch, wincing at the bloody mess he had made.

'Tina, Mr Chandralal's injury needs careful irrigation. I'll just get Dr Prince to check him over to see whether he's going to need to go upstairs or if we can deal with him down here. In the meantime, he's going to need a tetanus shot.'

She paused briefly at the door to make certain that Tina had recovered from her emotional outburst of the previous evening. In no time at all the young woman had confidently collected the supplies she would need and when she began explaining carefully to the elderly gentleman exactly what she was going to do Polly knew it was time to go in search of Nicholas Prince.

In spite of the fact that she had been on duty for over an hour, so far the consultant had been just a distant white-coated figure *en route* between examining rooms. Now she was going to see him face to face and she found herself strangely nervous.

'Idiot!' she muttered under her breath. 'He can't eat you, in spite of the fact you tried to call him to book last night.' She chuckled inwardly at the idea of a lowly junior sister having the temerity to tell a consultant off, but the humour of the situation faded as she remembered the empty vulnerability she had glimpsed when he'd told her of the reason behind his uneven temper.

'Busy enough?' she taunted softly when she caught up with him just as he dispatched an elderly stroke victim up towards the wards, the patient's tearful wife clutching his blue-veined hand as she accompanied his trolley towards the bank of lifts.

'Getting there.' He tilted his head towards her in wry acknowledgement, his grey eyes shadowed by bone-deep tiredness even at this early hour of his shift. 'Next time I open my big mouth remind me of the old saying—"Be careful what you wish for. . ."!'

'Well, I've got another one waiting for your expert assessment—a gentleman who stuck a garden fork through his foot.'

'Ouch,' he winced and turned to follow her while she continued talking.

'Because he was walking on it he's been bleeding like a stuck pig, but I don't think he hit anything major—unless he's done any nerve or tendon damage.'

'OK. Let's take a quick look. . .'

By the time they entered the treatment room Mr Chandralal was sitting forlornly on the examining couch, clutching his ruined shoe. Tina had obviously finished irrigating the injury to his foot and had covered it with a dry sterile dressing.

'Good girl,' Polly murmured quietly as the young woman stepped aside to allow the consultant to take her place.

'Well, Mr Chandralal,' Dr Prince said when he finally straightened up from his systematic examination of the elderly man's reflexes and functional responses, 'as far as I can tell, you haven't damaged any nerves or tendons in your foot, but the nature of the injury and the actual position means that you're going to be in quite a bit of pain while you're healing.'

'Thank you, Doctor,' he said fervently, tears of relief

making his dark eyes gleam. 'I am so sorry to have caused so much trouble.'

The consultant smiled briefly and Polly saw the fugitive creases at the corner of his eyes before he grew serious again.

'Well, if you don't mind me offering a word of advice, I think you would be wiser to wear something a little more substantial when you're gardening next time—maybe something with metal toecaps to give you some protection.'

Suddenly there was the harsh sound of an approaching siren and their heads all swivelled towards the sound.

Within seconds directions for the completion of Mr Chandralal's treatment had been given and hasty farewells had been made.

Polly's eyes followed the tall figure through the swing doors, then she dragged them back to the task in hand, quietly supervising Tina's careful work.

'You're doing well,' she encouraged when they were clearing the debris away, ready for the next patient.

'I'm just glad Dr Prince had to leave,' Tina said in a fervent aside. 'I was certain he'd end up shouting at me if he stayed to watch. I could feel myself beginning to shake, and I'm sure I'd have dropped everything on the floor.'

'I didn't know you were so badly affected by his good looks,' Polly deadpanned.

'His looks!' Tina squeaked, then realised that she was having her leg pulled. 'Sister! That's the *last* thing I think about when he's anywhere near me—although I suppose he isn't bad-looking for an older man.'

'Damned with faint praise!' Polly commented, then

grew serious again. 'You haven't had any further set-tos with him, have you?'

'Not since last night,' the young nurse confirmed. 'Mind you, I've been making certain that I keep well out of his way—he scares me!'

'He's only a man,' Polly said calmly, squashing down the memory of the semi-naked body she'd seen last night. 'He has to put his trousers on one leg at a time, the same as the rest of us!'

Tina giggled infectiously at the thought. 'Now I'll have to try to keep a straight face when he speaks to me.'

'That's better than quaking in your boots. Just make certain you're doing your job right and ask questions when you aren't certain.'

'Yes, Sister.'

'Sister Lang. . .?' a voice called from the other side of the swing doors, and Hannah Nicholls's dark head appeared. 'Big Mac wants to know if you're free to help Leo,' she murmured when Polly joined her by the door, quietly referring to the senior sister by her nickname. 'He's got a problem in room four with an OD.'

An overdose. . . Polly gave a little shudder of dread.

'I'll be right there, Hannah. . .'

She had no time to say any more before the head disappeared and the doors swung open smartly to admit a wheelchair, closely followed by a staff nurse and a rather green-looking junior doctor.

'I'll stay, shall I?' Tina volunteered gamely when she saw the blood-soaked cloth wrapped around the hand of the middle-aged man in the wheelchair.

'Good idea,' Polly agreed after a careful look at her determined expression, and swiftly left the room.

She just had time to signal her arrival to the diminutive martinet who was affectionately called Big Mac, and reached the doors of room four just as her nemesis approached them from the other direction.

'After you, sir,' she offered, flattening her palm against one door to push it open for him.

With a sharp glance and a brief murmur of thanks he strode into the room ahead of her.

'What's the problem, Leo?'

In the sudden silence that greeted his crisp voice Polly could have echoed his words, her eyes skimming over the disaster which seemed to have befallen the orderliness of the room. It was obvious from the spread of containers and equipment strewn around the floor that their patient had been strenuously resisting all offers of medical assistance. Finally her gaze came to rest on the unaccustomed expression of bemusement on Leo Stirling's handsome face.

'Problem?' a belligerent female voice answered, and they all found themselves following the shrill sound to the bedraggled figure on the examining table. 'There wouldn't *be* a problem if *he'd* only leave me alone. I don't *want* him to help me!'

The young woman glared fiercely at them, the expression in her reddened eyes reminding Polly of a cornered animal—or perhaps an injured one, afraid to believe that their assistance was kindly meant.

'But, Mrs Bishop. . . Sharron. . .' Leo obviously hadn't given up trying. 'If you won't let us help you you might die. . .'

'That's the whole bloody idea,' she swore, her voice slightly unsteady as it rose higher and higher. 'I *want* to die. . .I might just as well be dead. . .I'm no use as I am. . .'

The angry phrases degenerated into hopeless, helpless sobbing and Polly took the opportunity to hurry to the woman's side, one arm going around the heaving shoulders while the other reached for a handful of paper tissues.

'Here,' she offered gently, tightening her grip slightly to immobilise one arm when she felt the young woman stiffen and pressing the rustling white handful into her free hand.

For a second there was silence, as if everyone was holding their breath, before, with an unexpected, 'Thanks,' she used both hands to blow her running nose and scrub the streams of tears from her pale cheeks.

With no more than the lift of an eyebrow Nicholas Prince signalled to Polly, and when she nodded briefly in reply he silently gestured for the rest of the team to leave the room. Equally silently he crossed the room to position himself beside the swing doors so that he, too, was out of sight of their suicidal patient.

Polly breathed an inner sigh of relief that he was close enough to come to her help if necessary, and turned her attention back to her charge.

'Why can't they understand?'

The words were plaintive and sounded quite a bit more slurred than before.

'What don't they understand, Sharron?' Polly asked, knowing that the young woman's mental state wouldn't bear too much pushing but horribly conscious that time was ticking away.

'Why I don't want to be alive. . . No one understands. . . No one knows what it's like. . .inside. . . to know you're just a failure. . .'

As Polly tried to formulate another question two fat

tears spilled over and trickled down Sharron's pale cheeks.

'Man trouble?' she ventured.

'What else?' she slurred bitterly. 'They only 1-love you when you give them what they w-want, and if you can't. . .' She rolled her head against Polly's shoulder and looked up at her, defeat obvious in her expression. 'I. . .I can't give him a b-baby and he s-said. . .he said. . .'

The poor woman was unable to continue but Polly didn't need to hear the words to recognise her agony.

It didn't matter that in her own case it had been Tim's self-righteous condemnation and his impatience with her crippling guilt and fear which had destroyed their relationship and locked her emotions away inside.

'Shh. . . He's not worth it, Sharron,' Polly soothed, hoping against hope that she could find some common ground with the woman before the effect of drugs she'd taken became irreversible.

'How would you know?' Sharron challenged with a feeble burst of energy. 'You've got a good j-job. . . You've pro-probably got your own f-family.'

'No.' Polly shook her head sadly, fixing the young woman's gaze with her own and allowing the pain of all the memories to show. 'I'm divorced and he's remarried and starting a family.'

'Bastards. . .' Sharron hissed. 'They're all b-bastards. . .'

'But *I* decided I wasn't going to let the bastard win.' Polly repeated the epithet and shifted her grip so that she was holding Sharron by the shoulders. 'Don't *you* let him win, either,' she commanded fiercely. 'If he only wants you as a brood mare then he's ignorant and selfish and he's not worth killing yourself for. You're worth more than that.'

Sharron blinked at her owlishly, her thought processes slowing visibly as she tried to reason it all out.

''s right. . .' She nodded ponderously. 'Sh-selfish bastard. . .' Then she drew in a shuddering breath and gave a little whimper. 'I don't want to die. . . Please. . . Don't let me. . .die. . .' She closed her eyes and sagged forward against Polly's slender shoulder.

Instantly strong arms reached around her and relieved Polly of the weight as the swing doors flew open to admit the rest of the team.

'Airway,' Dr Prince's voice rapped as the limp body was stretched out and he wielded the first syringe. 'She needs a cuffed endotracheal tube before we can start to wash her out. Let's get that oxygen going. . .'

His words were almost superfluous as the team swung into its horribly familiar routine, the nasogastric tube swiftly positioned to allow the stomach to be lavaged.

'IV lifeline in,' Polly reported, relieved that she wasn't dealing with the collapsed veins of an habitual drugs user. 'Five per cent glucose going in.'

'Pinpoint pupils and respiratory depression,' Leo reported. 'Cardiac rhythm settling since you got the naloxone into her.'

'Do we know how much codeine she took?' Polly demanded when she saw the number of half-dissolved tablets being flushed up out of the young woman's stomach.

'Half a pharmacy, by the look of it. She certainly wasn't playing at it like some of them. It was sheer chance that her neighbour called round. This wasn't a cry for help, hoping to be found in time,' Dr Prince's voice broke in, his tone strangely flat.

'You're telling me,' Leo said with feeling as he sent blood samples up to the lab to check for drug concentration levels and flicked a glance across at Polly. 'She wouldn't let any of *us* touch her—fought like a wildcat. How did you do it?'

Polly felt the wash of heat over her cheek-bones as attention focused briefly on her, more conscious of a certain pair of wintry grey eyes than any others.

'Sometimes you just click,' she said dismissively. 'Some patients can relate better when they aren't surrounded by a crowd.' She made the mistake of allowing her gaze to travel across the trolley, but it wasn't until she was caught by the darkly knowing expression in Dr Prince's eyes that she remembered that he had been in the room when she'd been talking to Sharron and had heard everything she'd said.

Suddenly she couldn't remember exactly what she *had* said. How much had she told the young woman in her attempt at gaining her co-operation? How much had she said and how much had he gleaned of what she *hadn't* said?

'Sh-shall I find out if there's a side-ward bed she can go into?' Polly volunteered unsteadily when the first set of encouraging results came down from the lab, grabbing the first opportunity to put a little distance between the two of them to get her thoughts in order.

His agreement gave her the perfect excuse to leave the room and she contrived to take her first chance for a break immediately after the errand.

'He's being ever so quiet today,' Hannah commented under her breath as she offered the packet of biscuits.

'Who?'

'*Him,*' she said with a meaningful tilt of her head towards the door leading out into the department where, even as they spoke, they could hear the familiar deep tones of Nicholas Prince's voice.

'Oh. Good,' Polly said, deliberately taking a bite to excuse her lack of conversation on the subject. She usually shared her thoughts with Hannah and felt slightly guilty that she hadn't even mentioned the fact that she'd spoken to the consultant last night, much less that she'd visited him in his own home. In some strange way the whole episode had felt too personal to talk about, even to Hannah.

'I don't know if it is a good thing,' Hannah mused, pursing her lips thoughtfully. 'He's almost *too* quiet. You know—like a volcano just before it erupts. Well,' she continued with her usual good humour, 'if he does let's hope we get enough warning to evacuate the troops!'

Polly smiled at the joke, but she knew exactly what Hannah meant. So far today he *had* been strangely subdued and she had a bad feeling that it wasn't a good sign.

CHAPTER THREE

'HAVE you seen the notice?' Tina demanded eagerly as she slid the strap of her bag over her shoulder in preparation for going home.

'Notice?' Polly returned vaguely as she changed her shoes, preoccupied with the fact that not only had Dr Prince grown quieter and more withdrawn as the day had gone on but he had also left the hospital immediately his shift had ended. Although she had no right to be concerned, she was worried about him and wondered if she dared make a brief detour past his house now that she knew where he lived, to see if he. . .

'About the hospital fund-raiser.' Tina's voice intruded again.

Polly sighed silently and forced herself to concentrate, knowing that she would have to respond.

'Fund-raiser? When?' She glanced across at the cork noticeboard on the other side of the room and tried to see which one of the various brightly coloured posters had attracted Tina's attention.

'It's the Autumn Ball to raise money for the new whole-body scanner,' she elaborated, her young face alive with enthusiasm. 'This year, to help boost the funds, the committee have decided to combine the usual Ball with an Auction of Promises.'

'A what?' Finally Polly's attention was caught and she walked across to read the notice for herself.

'They want people to volunteer prizes for the auction,' Tina pointed out.

'Ohh,' Polly groaned. 'It'll end up being like some dreadful car boot sale, with everyone's worst Christmas presents up for sale.'

'Hardly, with prizes like a day's sailing in a twenty-five-foot yacht on offer,' Tina gloated.

'What?' Polly squeaked in amazement and looked more closely at the handwritten list below the announcement. 'Look! Someone's put up a week's accommodation in a holiday cottage in Brittany. . .and dancing lessons. . .'

'And a massage!' Tina giggled. 'I wonder if we get a choice of masseur—there's a really dishy bloke over in Physio that I wouldn't mind getting to grips with!'

'Tina!' Polly nearly choked. Was this the same tearful person she'd almost had to wring out last night? It was good to see how resilient she was—a quality much needed if she was determined to specialise in A and E.

They were both still laughing when they left the locker room to go home, but before they reached the exit doors Polly heard her name called with the clear precision of a Highland Scots accent.

'Yes, Sister,' she replied immediately and turned to answer the summons with a quiet, 'See you tomorrow,' for Tina.

'Dr Stirling tells me that your journey home takes you past Dr Prince's house,' Sister MacDonald announced in her usual no-nonsense manner. 'Unfortunately, after he left I found his wallet beside the chair in my office, and I would hate for him to think it was permanently lost. Would you be kind enough to drop it off for me?'

'Certainly, Sister. I'll take it straight away,' Polly agreed willingly, and tucked the well-worn leather folder into her own bag with a smile that barely hid her elation. She'd been wondering how she could possibly justify turning up on his doorstep again, without having to admit that she was worried about his mental state.

Now, out of the blue, she'd been handed a cast-iron reason for going to his house again. It might only take a few seconds for her to deliver his wallet, but she would be able to see him and set her mind at rest.

There were no lights on when Polly approached the house, in spite of the fact that the October evening was rapidly drawing in and the streetlights had started coming on. Anyway, she told herself, it didn't really signify anything—he could be in one of the rooms at the back of the house. . .

As she stepped forward to press the bell two things caught her attention almost simultaneously.

The fact that the heavy wooden front door hadn't been closed properly struck her as very strange, especially as she remembered the sound of the bolts he had drawn on her last visit, but it was the slight movement she caught out of the corner of her eye which made her blood run cold.

'Oh, God!' she breathed as her horrified gaze took in the sight visible around the edge of the open curtain.

There, in the sparsely furnished lounge, sat Nicholas Prince with a low wooden coffee-table in front of his chair and an array of guns spread out on the top of it. As she watched with her breath frozen in her throat he reached out a white-shirted arm to pick up a pistol and fit his finger around the trigger.

Suddenly it was as if her feet had grown wings and she whirled towards the front door and, without a thought for the social niceties, flung it open and raced inside.

'No! Nick. . .don't!' she called frantically as she
found the right door and pushed her way into the shad-
owy room where he was sitting. 'You can't. . .! You
mustn't. . .!' she protested as she stumbled to a halt just
inside the door.

He swung towards the intrusion and, in the stunned
silence which followed her outburst, Polly was sure that
the sound of her wild heartbeat must be reverberating
off the walls as his startled grey eyes stared at her over
the dully gleaming metal, the empty circle of the barrel
pointing straight at her like a malevolent eye.

'Please, Nick,' she pleaded in a shaky voice when
his aim remained unfalteringly on her. 'Please put it
down and think about it. . .talk about it.'

'It?' he echoed, seeming almost puzzled by
her words.

'The gun,' she whispered, as fear for him caused her
nails to score deeply into her palms, hardly daring to
take her eyes off him to look at the ugly thing. 'Will
you put it down while we talk about this?'

'The gun?' She saw him glance down at it almost
dismissively, then she saw his expression change to
utter disbelief as his eyes swung back up to hers. 'My
God! You didn't think I was going to. . .? Dammit,
you did!'

His incredulous tone brought her up sharply, its bite
more convincing than any words he could have used as
he thumped the weapon down on the table and straightened up to his full height.

Polly stood staring mutely up at him, the effects of
the adrenaline which had flooded through her system
leaving her with a sick trembling sensation deep inside,
her skin clammy enough to make her shudder in spite
of the warmth of her down-filled jacket.

'I'm sorry. . .' she mumbled when the uncomfortable silence seemed as if it would stretch into eternity, and she dragged her eyes away to gaze at the wall—at the furniture—anywhere except at him. 'I shouldn't. . .I didn't mean to. . .' She shrugged and fixed her eyes on the fringed edge of the slightly faded Indian carpet square centred on the polished parquet flooring just inches away from his naked feet.

'What's going on here?' he finally demanded, his harsh voice seeming too loud for her overstrained nerves. 'Why are you here? What gives you the right to come in here and insinuate that I. . .? How *did* you get in here in the first place?' He changed his angle of attack suddenly. 'I certainly didn't hear the bell.'

'The door wasn't shut.' Polly opted to answer the easiest question first, her voice thin and reedy-sounding after his powerful anger. 'I was just going to ring the bell when I saw that you must have left it open when you came in.'

'So you decided that gave you the right to march right in and throw accusations around?'

'No. . .'

She might as well have saved her breath because he wasn't listening.

'Well, I'm sorry I didn't realise that I had to be so careful about shutting doors,' he continued sarcastically, his hands clenching spasmodically as he raked her with eyes like honed steel. 'I obviously didn't know that it was an invitation to any passerby to invade my home and. . .'

'No. . . Please. . . It wasn't like that. . .' she burst out.

'Wasn't it?' he snapped. 'It seems to me that it was *exactly* like. . .'

'No, it's not! Here. . .' Before he could work up a

good head of steam Polly scrabbled in her bag, suddenly remembering the official reason why she had been standing on his doorstep in the first place. 'Sister MacDonald found this on the floor in her office but you'd already gone home.' She held out the well-worn leather object. 'She asked me to drop it in on my way home.'

In the ensuing silence Polly felt the guilt of half-truths heating her cheeks, and was grateful for the deepening gloom in the room when she remembered how delighted she'd been with the legitimate excuse to visit.

'My wallet,' he murmured after his hand reached back automatically for his trouser pocket and found it empty. 'I hadn't even realised it was gone. . .'

Silently Polly reached out to hand it to him but, instead of accepting it, he stepped forward and took the hand holding it between his own.

'I'm sorry,' he murmured contritely, but all Polly could concentrate on was the huskiness of his voice and the electric heat which travelled through her body like lightning from the contact between their hands.

'Will you forgive me for jumping to conclusions?' The huskiness in his deep voice affected her nerve endings like the insistent caress of a cat's tongue, and she had to drag her gaze away from its preoccupation with the way her own small pale hand was almost swallowed up in the lean strength of his.

'Pardon?' She blinked up at him, only managing to focus on what he was saying when she broke the contact between them by pulling her hand away. For several seconds all she'd been able to concentrate on was exactly how *much* she had cared that he might have been thinking of killing himself.

'Apologising to you seems to be becoming a regular

habit these days,' he said wryly as he slid both hands into his pockets. 'It's happening on a daily basis now.'

'Well, this time I need to apologise too,' she admitted as her eyes strayed towards the small array of weapons. 'It's just. . .I know from what you told me yesterday that you were dreading today, and at the hospital you seemed. . .withdrawn. . .' She let the words die away as she shrugged.

'So you added two and two?'

'Well, what would *you* have thought if you'd glanced towards a window and seen someone pick up a gun and point it at himself?' Polly demanded. 'I didn't even know that you kept guns, or I'd have. . .' She stopped speaking and bit her tongue, suddenly aware that the words hovering on its tip would have revealed just how worried she had been about him—just how much she had started to care for this taciturn man.

'They were my father's,' he volunteered and turned towards the table again, scooping up the small case lying on the floor beside it. 'When he died several years ago I transferred them to my name—nostalgia, I suppose—and locked them securely away. I'd all but forgotten I had them until I heard something on the radio earlier on. . .I was just cleaning them one last time before I surrender them at the local police station.'

As he was speaking he paused with his hand over the switch on the small table lamp, then glanced towards the open curtains. When he left the room in near dark-ness Polly guessed that he had realised that it was safer to finish what he was doing without giving any passerby the chance to see into the room.

Moving with his customary swift efficiency, he slot-ted each weapon into its own recessed slot in the case and then did the same with a small steel box and several anonymous lumps of metal.

'What are they?' Polly was intrigued in spite of herself and took a step closer.

'The firing mechanisms for each of those.' He nodded towards the guns. 'Each is useless without the other so I take them apart and secure them separately so that even if I'm burgled it's unlikely that both parts will be taken.'

'And you'd already taken them apart before I arrived?' Polly guessed, feeling more stupid with every passing minute.

'That's right,' he confirmed and she thought she saw the brief gleam of his smile as he glanced up at her. 'So, when you saw me, not only was I holding a gun without a firing mechanism but I don't even possess any ammunition.'

'Well, at least when I make a fool of myself I do a good job of it,' Polly said in a strangled voice, knowing that he was laughing at her—knowing that he thought she was a fool. 'But now that I've delivered your wallet I'd better be on my way home.'

'Polly. . .' His voice halted her at the door. 'You know, you didn't make a fool of yourself. It was actually a very brave thing to do.'

'Brave?' The word surprised her. She hadn't thought of it like that. . .hadn't expected him to think like that. All she'd been conscious of at the time was the fact that she hadn't wanted him to do something so destructive while he was depressed. She had the feeling that real bravery was what she would be needing a large measure of when she had to face him in the morning when she went on duty.

'Yes. Brave,' he insisted, as if he could hear the

argument going on inside her head. 'What if the gun *had* been loaded? I could easily have killed you too.'

She considered the idea briefly and shook her head.

'No. You couldn't,' she said with utter conviction. 'You're too good a doctor to waste a life like that.'

There was a long silence before he gave a short bark of laughter.

'At least, not intentionally,' he agreed with a depressingly swift return to bitterness. 'It doesn't mean that people don't end up just as dead.'

Polly had an idea that she knew only too well what he meant, but she knew that she daren't comment as she listened to the sounds as he picked up the case. She could only dimly perceive his movements in the light that seeped into the room from the streetlamps, and suddenly realised just how dark it had grown since she had pushed her way into his house.

'I'm sorry,' she murmured, not knowing what else she could say, and reached for the door. 'Well, I. . .I'll see you tomorrow, then.'

'Stay. . .'

The word was hardly more than a husky whisper but she heard it as clearly as if he had shouted it, and her breath stopped in her throat. What exactly was he asking?

'Please. . .'

They were both standing still in the darkened room, his face nothing more than a paler shadow among shadows, but she could remember all too clearly the desolation in his expression when he'd told her that his wife was dead.

'But. . . Dr Prince. . .'

'Nick,' he prompted softly.

'Pardon?'

'You called me Nick when you thought I was going to blow my brains out,' he reminded her, and she felt the heat rise in her cheeks. She'd used his name unconsciously and had hoped that he hadn't noticed the slip.

'Yes, well, that was. . .it was. . .'

'Please. I need someone to talk to—someone who'll understand.'

How did he know the one argument which she couldn't refuse, much as she knew she should?

'But I. . .'

'Just for a little while?'

Polly closed her eyes tightly as she fought to ignore the little voice inside her head which was telling her to leave. She knew that it was the sensible thing to do, but when had she ever been able to make her head rule her soft heart?

'All right,' she agreed. 'Just for a little while.'

For several seconds he was silent, as if he couldn't believe what she'd said, then she heard him release a deep sigh.

'I need to lock these away.' He lifted the case of guns. 'Would you like to go through to the kitchen, or. . .'

'The kitchen's fine,' she interrupted hastily. 'I could put the kettle on, if you like.' She pulled the door open and stepped out into the hallway, then came to a full stop.

The fanlight window over the front door allowed a small band of streetlight into the hallway, but it didn't reach far enough to show her the way to the kitchen door.

'Light switch on the wall to your left,' he murmured, and she squeaked as his voice sounded right beside her ear.

'You made me jump,' she complained as she fumbled

across the cool expanse of freshly painted wall in search
of the elusive switch. 'I didn't hear you move.'

There was a sharp click as she found it, and the
hallway was flooded with brightness.

'Sorry to startle you,' he apologised, 'but it's a bit
difficult to make a lot of noise with bare feet.'

Polly could hear the hint of laughter in his voice and
refused to look, hurrying towards the door at the end
of the hallway as if her life depended on it.

She had made a pot of tea and was just about to pour
it out into two mugs when she suddenly remembered
his reaction to the beverage last night. Swiftly she took
the teapot over to the sink, but before she could pour
it away and substitute coffee he was there.

'Ah, good. Did you find everything you needed?'

He scooped the two mugs up off the table and brought
them towards her, a quick glance inside showing him
that she'd already put milk in each.

'No. . . Yes. . . I. . .I'm sorry, Doctor. . .'

'Nick,' he reminded her. 'You were going to call me
Nick, remember?'

'Nick,' she echoed, then dragged in a shaky breath
and forced herself to face him. 'I'm sorry. . . Nick. . .
but I forgot about. . .I forgot that you can't. . .I made
tea,' she finished lamely. 'It won't take a minute for
the kettle to boil again for coffee. . .'

'No,' he said sharply and pressed his lips tightly
together and started again in a calmer tone. 'No. It's
quite all right, Polly. It's time I started consciously
putting it behind me, and the first step might as well
be a cup of tea.'

He deposited the mugs on the draining-board and
waited while she poured in the tea, then took charge of
them again as he led the way back into the sitting-room,

drawing the curtains and switching on the table lamp in the corner before inviting her to sit.

When he settled himself down in the other corner of the enormous squashy settee and angled his long legs towards her own she suddenly became aware that the two of them were closer now than they'd ever been before—closer and totally alone, without the possibility of interruption from other members of staff.

Nervously she directed her eyes away from him, determined to make a minute inspection of her surroundings rather than allow herself to notice the way the soft light highlighted the golden gleam of his rumpled hair or outlined the angles and planes of his face.

In the mellow lamplight the room no longer looked stark and bare—in fact, now that she looked more closely, she could see that everything looked freshly decorated.

'You've been having a lot of work done in the house,' she commented brightly, trying to fill the suffocating silence which seemed to have fallen between them like a thick grey mist. 'Is it nearly finished?'

'It'll be a while yet—the downstairs rooms are all but finished, but I've only just begun upstairs.'

'You?' Polly's eyes widened. 'You mean you've been doing the work yourself?'

'As much as I can,' he admitted. 'I decided for safety's sake to leave things like wiring and plastering to the professionals, but as for the rest. . .' he shrugged '. . .I quite enjoy the challenge.'

'The kitchen, too?' Polly demanded, her admiration making her forget that she'd been determined not to look at him. She'd taken a real delight in exploring the design and finish of the beautiful fitted cupboards while she'd made their tea. 'All those fantastic cabinets?'

'Made them and installed them,' he confirmed, with more than a touch of justified pride in his voice.

Polly was quite speechless at the scope of his talent and patience. Knowing how many hours he had been spending at the hospital and seeing the result of many hours of labour here, it was no wonder that he was short-tempered and exhausted. He could hardly have been sleeping at all. . .

'I'm impressed,' she said finally, with massive under-statement. 'And you're working your way right through the house?'

'Room by room—do you want to see how far I've got?'

He straightened up eagerly out of his corner and held out his hand to pull her up out of the comfortable embrace of the deep upholstery.

The contact between them was brief, but Polly was conscious of a strange residual tingling in her hand after he'd effortlessly set her on her feet, and she was careful to keep enough distance between them to avoid any accidental contact as he led the way through the quiet elegance of the ground-floor rooms.

'I love the mixture of furniture you've chosen,' she commented as they ended up in the hallway again. 'The pieces you've made yourself complement the older ones very well.' She smiled up at him, marvelling at how easy the atmosphere had become between them.

'It's not the same up here,' he warned as he padded his way up the freshly polished bare treads in his equally bare feet. 'The house was owned by an elderly man and he'd been unable to go upstairs for several years before he finally had to sell.'

'I see what you mean,' she said, screwing up her

nose at the grim dinginess of the upstairs hallway. It seemed so much worse after the beauty they'd just left downstairs.

'And that's *after* I've scrubbed everything down,' he pointed out ruefully as he pushed open the first door at the top of the stairs and flicked the switch to light the bare bulb hanging in the centre of the room. 'There are two more like this.'

'What had you planned doing with them?'

Once she got over the appalling state of decoration she could see that the proportions of the room were good and her imagination started working.

'Probably pretty much the same as down there.' He tilted his head towards the stairs. 'The floors aren't in the same good condition up here because the original timber wasn't of the same quality so I'll probably have to carpet them, but apart from that. . .'

After seeing what he had achieved downstairs she could easily picture what the doors and windows would look like once he'd stripped the chipped paint, finished the wood underneath to a soft golden shine and painted the freshly plastered walls.

'I've nearly finished in here. . .' He pushed open the next door to reveal a partially tiled bathroom, the pile of boxes in the corner proving that eventually the rest of the walls would be covered with the same creamy onyx tiles that surrounded the bath and shower.

'Is that as far as you've gone?' she said, almost disappointed to have come to the end of the tour. She'd thoroughly enjoyed being shown round his home and seeing the work he'd put into its restoration. It had given her an insight into a totally unexpected side of the reserved man she thought she'd known.

She didn't know whether it was her imagination, but

he seemed to hesitate briefly before he indicated the last door.

'Only this one,' he said as he pushed the door wide with sudden determination and flicked the switch. 'My room.'

Polly hung back for a second, her cheeks flushing as the significance struck her, but overwhelming curiosity forced her to step forward.

It was a very masculine room, full of natural wood and earth tones from pale oatmeal to the rich depth of terracotta and bitter chocolate, the furniture scaled to fit his height.

'It's lovely,' she said honestly and smiled at him—anything to keep her eyes away from the smooth expanse of the magnificent polished wood double bed. Then he returned her smile, and with an instantaneous leap in her pulse she realised that she could see behind the withdrawn façade to the person walled up inside the pain.

Suddenly it wasn't just the bed she couldn't look at—it was the man standing beside her. What on earth was she doing in his bedroom, for heaven's sake?

In their busy quest for something to look at her eyes alighted on a small silver frame on top of the tallboy beside her, and before she could stop herself she'd reached out and turned it towards her.

'Oh. . .!' she breathed when she saw the image of a much younger, happier Nick Prince, laughing as he tried to shield his beautiful new wife from a shower of confetti.

Polly shut her eyes tightly, horrified by what she had done—and today of all days.

The silence went on and on and she wished that the

floor would simply open up and swallow her. How could she possibly apologise?

'Our wedding day,' he confirmed needlessly, his voice sounding as painful as if it were travelling over rough gravel, and he reached out to touch the photo gently with the tip of one lean finger before he clenched his hand and pulled it away again. 'We met when Dee was in her final year of nursing training.'

'Please. . .' Polly turned and reached a tentative hand out towards him. It was tearing her apart inside, just hearing him talk about it—hearing the pain in his voice. What must it be doing to him? What must it be like for him to drag all the memories out? 'Nick, you don't have to tell me.'

'Yes, I do,' he said, suddenly fierce as he gripped her hand. 'Please, Polly, I need to talk about it—to tell you. . .'

She gazed up into his face and saw the pain bracketing his mouth and shadowing his eyes and nodded.

'We'd been married for four years before we were ready to start a family, and couldn't believe it when we were successful on our first attempt.' His smile was almost bashful and she saw a hint of colour wash along his cheek-bones.

'For safety's sake, we waited until she'd got past the twelve-week stage and was just beginning to show before we went to visit her parents to break the news— only we never got there. Some drunk tried to beat the traffic lights and ploughed right into her side of the car.'

'Oh, God,' Polly breathed, longing to comfort him— longing to wrap her arms around him to let him know that he wasn't alone—but she had a feeling that this was the first time that he had allowed himself to talk about it, and knew from the tension in his body that there was more to come so she didn't dare move.

'She was trapped,' he whispered, his wintry grey eyes so desolate as he gazed down at her that she knew he wasn't seeing her but the memories which haunted him. 'The two cars were so tangled together that they had to cut them apart to get to her, and all the time the drunk was cursing and swearing about his no-claims bonus while she was bleeding to death.'

He closed his eyes and a solitary tear spilled over and ran down his cheek.

'Oh, Nick. . .'

Finally she dared to reach up and wrap her arms around him, one hand cupping the back of his bent head. For just a second he resisted, then his own arms wrapped convulsively around her and the sobs shook his broad shoulders.

The storm was brief but fierce, and when he would have turned away in embarrassment at having let down the barriers so comprehensively Polly calmly handed him the man-sized handkerchief from her pocket and suggested that a cold flannel would soothe his eyes.

She avoided looking at him, hoping to allow him enough time to regain control, and when she heard the soft whisper of his bare feet leaving the room she busied herself by folding back the covers on his bed.

For a moment she contemplated going back down to the kitchen to heat some milk, but before she could carry the idea out she heard him returning.

'I'd better be going. . .'

'I'm sorry. . .'

They both began to speak together and broke off in confusion.

'There's nothing to apologise for,' she said firmly, saddened when she saw the way he was avoiding her eyes. 'I expect you'd have done the same thing for me if the positions had been reversed. I'm just glad that I was here for you. Perhaps it would be a good idea if you tried to catch up on some sleep?'

He glanced at the prepared bed and chuckled wryly. 'Not something I can do a lot of these days,' he commented tellingly. 'I've been here for nearly a year and the house has never seemed so big and empty as it has the last few weeks.'

'I can remember that feeling,' Polly said. 'I even resorted to leaving music playing.'

'Did it work?'

She shook her head. 'The only thing that helped was when a friend's marriage was going through a sticky patch. She came to stay while she thought things through, and just the presence of another person. . .'

'Will you stay for me?'

The sudden request shocked her so much that she thought she must have misheard him, her eyes widening in disbelief.

'Stay?' she whispered, while her heart stumbled and her breath caught in her throat.

'Just to talk. . .just so there's someone there,' he pleaded softly. 'If I don't get some sleep soon. . .' He closed his eyes tiredly and sighed.

She looked at the lines of exhaustion marking his face and all her sensible objections flew out of the window.

'I could stay for a while,' she conceded, 'but I'll need to get some sleep myself if I'm going to be any use tomorrow. If you like, I could make you some hot chocolate while you get yourself settled.'

As soon as he agreed she made her way swiftly down the stairs, firmly squashing the nervous skip in her pulse when she had a mental image of his powerful body sliding between the crisp cotton covers.

For safety's sake, she gave him nearly ten minutes before she made her careful way back up the stairs with a steaming mug in each hand.

He'd piled the pillows against the polished wood of the headboard and the bedside light was gilding the curve of one shoulder when she approached him, her eyes carefully focused on the unsteady surface of the liquid rather than on the broad expanse of naked chest in front of her.

'Thank you, Sister,' he said with a self-mocking grimace as he accepted her offering. 'I can't remember how many years it's been since I had a hot milky drink at bedtime, but at this point I'm willing to try almost anything.'

He screwed up his nose like a sulky little boy as he took the first sip, and Polly chuckled at the startled expression which came over him.

'Now *that's* what I call a milky drink,' he said with a smile as he took a second larger mouthful. 'I take it you found the brandy bottle.'

'And lowered the level in it,' she agreed with an answering smile as she sipped her own drink.

'Did you put some in yours too?'

'No way! I'd fall asleep standing up if I was to drink any,' she joked as she transferred her weight uneasily from one foot to the other while her gaze flickered from his bed to the chair full of clothes which stood almost at the edge of the circle of light.

'Well, then, the least you can do is take the weight off your feet and get yourself comfortable.' He patted the bedclothes beside him in invitation. 'There's plenty of room.'

'Oh, but. . .'

'Tell me,' he continued, completely overriding her attempted objection, 'what do you think of the way the new system's working in A and E? What sort of feedback are you getting from the rest of the staff?'

Polly was so startled by the abrupt change in pace of the conversation that before she realised it she was sharing the pile of pillows and was in the middle of a heated discussion about staffing levels and emergency recall procedures in the event of a large-scale disaster.

It must have been nearly an hour later that she realised that Nick's pause for thought had turned into genuine sleep when his head came to rest heavily against her shoulder.

'Nick?' she whispered, loath to disturb him but she needed to go home.

Over the space of the last hour the two of them had gradually slid down so that it should have been a simple matter for her to extricate herself from his trusting weight. Unfortunately, as soon as she tried to move away he muttered something unintelligible and rolled over to face her, one muscular arm draping across her to pin her more firmly in position than ever.

CHAPTER FOUR

POLLY had no idea what time it was when she woke up. All she knew was that it was still dark outside.

For several seconds she hadn't even been able to work out where she was but when she tried to turn over and found herself held firmly against a solid, naked body she remembered.

'Nick?' she whispered as she tried to lift his arm off her ribs, but all he did was tighten his grip so that her back was plastered against his chest, his face burrowing into the curve beneath her ear with a husky murmur.

'Nick?' She tried again, accompanying the word with a wriggle as she tried to slide out from under his hold, but when his hand closed convulsively around the softness of one breast she froze.

For more than a minute she lay absolutely still, her mind refusing to find a solution to her predicament as it took delight in cataloguing her every reaction to his touch.

Her breathing had grown rapid and her pulse jumped as her sleep-warmed flesh revelled in the touch of his hand, tinglingly aware of each long finger as they cupped her swelling roundness.

He lay motionless behind her, his even breathing teasing the back of her neck, but just when she thought he must have returned to deep sleep his hand moved again, his fingers flexing against the revealing hardness of her nipple so that she nearly moaned aloud.

'Mmm,' he murmured huskily, moving restlessly

behind her, and suddenly, as his thighs brushed against the backs of her legs, she was shocked to realise that she was no longer lying on top of the bedclothes. At some time while she'd been asleep she had ended up sharing his covers.

'Nick!' she whispered again, her scurrying heartbeat lending an edge of panic to her voice as his fingers probed the opening between the buttons on her blouse and discovered the silky heat of her naked breast.

'Beautiful,' he whispered, his voice deep and husky with sleep as he teased and taunted her aroused flesh with knowing fingers. 'Ah, sweetheart, come here. . .' And he rolled her towards him and took possession of her mouth.

For several seconds shock robbed her of the instinct to fight but by that time his tongue had insinuated itself inside her mouth, and when her own greeted the intruder with a sinuous dance of welcome she knew she was lost.

Somewhere in the back of her mind a small voice was trying to tell her that this was wrong, but when he lifted his head briefly to gaze down at her all she could see was that he needed her, desperately, and when he found the swollen slick evidence of her own blatant desire all she wanted to do was wrap her arms around him and welcome him into her body.

'Thank goodness for half-days,' Polly murmured as she changed out of her uniform the next day.

'And quiet shifts,' agreed Hannah as she prepared to go back on duty. 'Although why I'm pleased that it was quiet for you, I don't know. The second half of my shift will probably be bedlam! Still, at least I've got a late start tomorrow so think of me when you have to get up in the morning. . .' She waved a cheeky goodbye and left Polly to her thoughts.

She'd been lucky so far today. The second time she'd woken up she'd only just had time to dash home and dive under the shower before it had been time to go to work. Lucky, too, that Nick hadn't had to go to work until later, and that he'd still been sleeping so heavily that she hadn't disturbed him when she'd slid out of the wildly rumpled bed.

She hadn't been able to resist pausing at the door of his room for one last look at him, storing up in her mind the magnificent picture of the powerful symmetry of his body sprawled bonelessly across the bed, his modesty unnecessarily protected by one corner of the sheet.

Her cheeks burnt as she realised where her eyes were fixed and she dragged them away to look at his face.

The thick old-gold strands of his hair were tousled boyishly across his forehead, all the lines of stress and tension smoothed out so that he looked years younger. His thick, much darker lashes threw fan-like shadows onto his cheeks, temporarily hiding the darker shadows which insomnia had caused to grow there over the last few weeks.

His jaw was heavily darkened by his early-morning beard, and her breasts tingled as she remembered the sensuous rasp of it over her tender flesh while he'd explored them.

One arm was flung up over his head, displaying the strangely vulnerable tuft of darker hair, and the other lay across the space she had so recently vacated, the fingers loosely curled as though he had been reaching out for her in his sleep.

Part of her longed to join him there—to wake him

up and lose herself once more in the glory of his love-making—but the saner half knew that it wasn't possible.

She knew that, in spite of the fact that he'd been blameless, even after two years he was still racked by grief over the death of his wife and unborn child and wasn't ready to welcome anyone else into his life.

Anyway, she reminded herself, she knew how much it hurt to cry for the moon, and she'd promised herself that she wouldn't put herself through that again.

She shivered in the early morning autumn chill, dreading their first encounter. He probably wouldn't even need to say anything to make her blush from head to toe. Just one look from those molten steel eyes would be enough to turn her bones to jelly, especially when she remembered the way he had looked at her when he'd taken possession of her body. . .

'It's no good thinking about it when you know it's safer all round if the two of us put the whole episode behind us,' she muttered as she picked up her bag and started walking along the hospital corridor, scowling at the thought that before she could catch up on her sleep she'd got the shopping to do on the way home then the laundry and. . .

'Polly.'

One husky word stopped her in her tracks and her heart felt as if it was going to leap right out of her chest.

She turned to face him, her eyes flicking nervously from side to side to see who might be watching.

'Dr Prince,' she greeted him, her eyes firmly fixed on the broad burgundy stripe in his tie. She didn't dare look up into his face—even thinking about it was flooding her face with heat.

'It's Nick, remember,' he said in the same slightly roughened tone he'd used last night when he'd finally caught his breath enough to cradle her against his side and murmur endearments.

He took a step closer, and when she tried to retreat she found herself neatly backed against the wall. 'You should have woken me before you left,' he complained, his intonation making every nerve ending tingle as if he were stroking her with velvet.

'I had to go home to change for work.' She tried to be prosaic in an attempt at controlling her reaction to him. She was uncomfortable talking about the episode at all, never mind that the conversation was taking place in a busy corridor.

'I would still have liked. . .'

'Anyway, you needed your sleep,' she butted in, desperately wishing that she'd left the hospital just two minutes earlier. Then this conversation would never have taken place. 'There was no point in waking you up just to say goodbye.'

'It would have been more than just goodbye, Polly.' He leant towards her and she felt surrounded by him, drawing in the indefinable mixture of soap and skin which could only be Nicholas Prince.

'But. . .'

She was totally flustered. Ever since she'd first met him he'd always been slightly withdrawn, and she'd always thought it was a result of the responsibilities heaped on his shoulders.

This Nicholas Prince was a stranger and she had no idea why he was behaving like this towards her—and in such a public place. Although this area was officially out of bounds to members of the public, staff could appear at any time and heaven only knew what they'd have made of the scene that confronted them. Had he lost all respect for her after she'd fallen into his arms so easily?

When her thoughts finally spiralled to a halt she realised that he'd been staring down at her in silence for some time and heat washed up her throat again.

'We need to talk, Polly.'

He straightened away from the wall and took a step back, and she nearly made a run for it, her heart starting to thump like a startled rabbit's again.

'T-talk?'

She'd only stayed to talk last night, and look what had happened. . .

'I should be finished by eight tonight. Can I take you out for a meal?'

It had been phrased as a question, but inside she quivered when she recognised the steely determination behind it.

Before she could dig an answer out of her paralysed brain the corridor was filled with the shrill sound of his pager.

'Dammit. . .' He silenced it with a frustrated stab of one finger and then leant towards her again, for the first time touching her as he raised her chin with the tip of the same finger.

Polly couldn't resist. Her gaze slid inexorably up over the neatly tied knot in his tie and the tanned column of his throat, pausing briefly as she fought to subdue the memories of what that mouth had felt like when it had possessed her own with such fervour, until at last she met the burning intensity of his eyes.

How could she ever have thought that grey eyes were cold when his seared her like molten steel with a single glance?

'Polly.' His deep voice was huskier than ever and

the sound sent a shiver right up her spine. 'We *do* need to talk—the sooner the better,' he continued, dragging her thoughts back from their heated wanderings. 'I'll see you as close to eight as I can make it.'

As he straightened up again, allowing a few more inches between their bodies, Polly began to draw in a silent breath of relief that the encounter was over, but she'd relaxed too soon. Before she'd realised what he intended to do he'd swooped down again and kissed her, the warmth of his lips lingering just long enough to brand her with his touch.

Before she could even think about whether she should reject the contact or respond to it he was gone, his long legs eating up the distance as he hurried towards the nearest phone.

Reaction still had Polly's legs quivering like jelly, and she had to lean weakly against the wall for several minutes while she gathered her thoughts enough to make for the nearest exit.

'Ah, Polly. . . Light of my life!' Leo called after her, and Polly groaned as she turned to face him. Was she never going to escape?

'Hello, Leo. What do *you* want?' she said, softening the exasperation in her question with a smile.

'Don't be like that.' He feigned hurt. 'You know I only have eyes for you.'

'And the rest!' Her grin was starting to feel more natural, his nonsense managing to bring her feet back to the ground far faster than a fight with a trolley in the local supermarket. 'What is it this time?'

'Well, it's about the Autumn Ball or, to be more accurate, the Auction part.'

Polly frowned. 'I don't see how I can help. I'm not quite in the same league as the consultants who are offering holidays in Brittany or sailing on a yacht.'

'Actually, that's why I needed to talk to you. Have you got a minute?'

'So much for getting all my chores done and catching up on some sleep,' she moaned, pulling a wry face. 'All right. But only on conditio. that we find somewhere to sit outside. I'm late going off duty as it is, and I refuse to stay inside this building one minute longer.'

'And I bet you haven't eaten either. Hang on, then. Let's make a quick detour.' He grabbed her elbow and directed her towards the coffee-shop, plying a steady trade in one corner of the enormous ultramodern foyer.

Within minutes a blushing matronly volunteer had succumbed to his good looks and cheerful charm and he was paying for a selection of freshly cut sandwiches and fruit and two lidded containers of orange juice.

'Any preferences for the venue?' he demanded as they jogged out of the way of an ambulance which was turning towards the nearby outpatients block.

'How about the grassy area behind the special care baby unit? There's a wooden bench under the trees.'

'Your every wish is my command, fair lady,' he declared, and led the way.

'So, Leo, what's the problem?' Polly prompted when she'd finished tucking all the empty wrappings into one paper bag and turned to face him, one arm resting along the back of the wooden bench. 'If you're looking for me to provide you with a star prize you're out of luck. It's all a bit out of my league, I'm afraid.'

'That's the problem in a nutshell,' he admitted in a worried tone. 'I was absolutely delighted at first when people were so generous but it wasn't long before the murmurs started.'

'Murmurs?'

'That there wasn't going to be anything of interest for the majority.'

'You mean the rest of the plebs, like me, who would never dare to bid on tickets to a West End show when they know they're up against the financial muscle power of a consultant?'

'Exactly! And now that I've backed myself into a corner I can't see how to get myself out of it.' He ran the fingers of one hand distractedly through his thick tawny hair.

'Embarrassing, especially as, by all accounts, the whole thing was your idea in the first place.'

'Don't remind me!' he groaned as he straightened up and sat back against the bench, mirroring her own position.

The sullen grey light of an autumn afternoon struggled its way through the almost leafless branches of the tree behind them to play over his lean body as he glowered in the direction of the massive new wing of the hospital.

Polly was silent for a moment, thinking, but nothing immediately came to mind.

'Have you got a list of the promises so far? Perhaps that will give us an idea?'

'Here you are. . .' Leo leant towards her as he fished in his pocket to pull out several sheets of paper folded together. 'The list so far. I've read it so often I'm beginning to have nightmares about it!'

Polly skimmed her way down it with an appreciative whistle. 'Wow! What a fantastic haul! You should be able to raise quite a bit towards the scanner with this little lot.'

'But only if there are enough people with deep enough pockets to bid for them,' he complained in despair. 'If everything goes too cheaply it'll seem like an insult to the people who have made such generous donations, but the majority of the people at the Ball won't get a look-in if the prices are too high.'

The offer of a massage caught Polly's eye and she smiled as she remembered the way Tina Wadland had coveted it—especially if she had her choice of masseur.

Suddenly she had a glimmer of an idea and she straightened up sharply, leaning forward to rest her elbows on her knees as she scanned the list again.

'Have you got a pen?' she demanded, her eyes fixed on the paper propped on her knees as she started reading from the top again.

'Here.' Leo handed her one then leant over her to see what she was doing. 'What have you got?' he queried hopefully as he rested one arm around her shoulders.

'Just an idea. Give me a minute while I. . .' She concentrated fiercely, the pen swooping at intervals to add notations down the side of the page, before she straightened up again. 'Listen to this. . .'

She read out a partial list of the wonderful prizes people had promised and Leo's face grew longer.

'So?' he challenged. 'As I said, people have been very generous.'

'Now listen to these. . .' She began reading again, but this time, instead of the 'star' prizes, she listed such items as the massage—with Tina's comment about her preferences—and the offer of dancing lessons—with an aside about Fred Astaire's understudy being available if Patrick Swayze couldn't make it after all. . .

'Give me that!' There was a current of excitement in his voice as he reached out and snatched the list from her hand, his eyes skimming quickly down the items she'd marked and he whooped. 'You marvellous woman! I think you've cracked it!' He flung both arms around her and delivered a smacking kiss.

Polly laughed aloud at his boyish exuberance.

Out of the corner of her eye she saw an anonymous, tall, white-coated figure pause by one of the huge plate-glass windows in the overlooking corridor, and her heart leapt with the thought that it might be Nick.

Suddenly one small corner of her mind marvelled that a kiss and a hug from this gorgeous specimen of virile male did absolutely nothing for her, while all she had to do was *think* about the husky tone in the voice of a certain A and E consultant and her pulse went haywire.

She dragged her concentration back to the matter in hand.

'As far as I can see, Leo, all you need to do is make sure that you mix the fun items among the swanky ones and play the humour of the situation for all you're worth. You might need a few more of the light-hearted items. . .'

'*That* won't be a problem now I know what I'm looking for!' he exclaimed animatedly. 'In fact, it might even be an idea if we had one or two prizes that were outside the auction itself—perhaps a raffle prize or a draw of the Ball tickets. . .' His voice faded away and she could see that his mind was racing on at full speed, his tawny eyes getting a faraway look as he forgot that she was there.

'Well, sir.' Polly gathered up her belongings and got to her feet, wrapping her jacket around her as a chilly breeze caught her and made her shiver. 'Now that I've solved your problem, please may I go? There's a super-market trolley just waiting to wrench my arms out of their sockets and a washing machine that can't wait to chew my clothes up and help all the colours to run together.'

'Oh, Polly, I'm sorry,' Leo apologised ruefully as he dragged himself away from his planning and straightened up to his full six feet, apparently unconcerned that the same breeze had tousled his hair and heightened the colour in his cheeks. 'You've been a wonderful help, sweetheart. I'd never have seen the solution if you hadn't pointed it out. I'll show you how far I've got when you have a break tomorrow.'

He leant forward to plant another swift kiss on her cheek and then loped away across the grass, turning to call over his shoulder, 'How about eleven o'clock, and you can make the coffee. . .?'

'OK. It's a date,' she agreed laughingly, then watched as he paused long enough to offer a gentlemanly elbow to an elderly lady struggling out of a taxi and steadied her on her feet.

Polly shook her head as she made her way towards the shops, stepping out briskly to minimise the effects of the dismal day. It was hard to realise that Leo and Nick were within a few years of each other in age. Oh, they were both excellent A and E doctors and had apparently known each other for some years, but Leo was such a live wire that he seemed far younger—as if life had yet to make its mark on him.

Whereas Nick. . . The excitement stirred inside her when she thought about his unexpected invitation, only slightly tempered by the quiver of apprehension she felt about his insistence that they needed to talk. He'd seemed so serious, as if. . .

She forced out an exasperated breath when she realised that she had just walked past the entrance to the supermarket, and resolved to make herself concentrate on the chores she still had to do before she could think about getting ready.

In spite of frequent stern reminders, she couldn't help her thoughts wandering as she tried to decide what to wear.

In the few seconds available in the corridor he'd given her no idea where he was going to take her, and she had an awful mental picture of opening her door dressed to the nines to find Nick on the step in jeans and a casual jumper.

Then she couldn't decide if it would be worse if the situation were reversed and she ended up sitting in a very smart restaurant with an escort in a three-piece suit and an expensive pure silk tie, while she wore leggings and a voluminous jumper.

By the time eight o'clock came round she was a nervous wreck. It seemed to have taken her hours of trying on and discarding before she'd settled on her favourite heavy silk pleated evening trousers and a wrap-over jade silk blouse, and it had taken her another age to put away the rest of her wardrobe so that the flat was tidy again before he was due to arrive.

One part of her was insisting piously that it didn't matter if she left the bedroom in a mess because Nick was only coming to take her out so that they could talk and would therefore not see if the room was tidy.

The other, more hopeful part was alive with the possibility that if the evening went well Nick might very well see the inside of her bedroom when he returned her home later tonight. . .

She glanced around the room to feverishly check one last time that everything was neat and tidy, her eyes skimming over the African violet just coming into flower on the window-sill and the ticket to the Autumn

Ball which she had propped up on the mantelpiece just behind the photo. . .

Her eyes, her thoughts, her breathing, *everything* slammed to a halt when she focused on the precious oblong, framed in silver, which gleamed softly in the subdued lighting.

She took a step towards it, her hand shaking slightly as she reached out a finger to stroke the image tenderly.

In the stillness of the room she clearly heard the clock chime the hour as a car drew up outside the building, and she dragged her eyes away from the photo to look out of the window, smiling at Nick's punctuality. . . only it wasn't Nick who got out of the car which had parked under the streetlight outside. The man was a stranger who waved and called a greeting as one of the other tenants in the subdivided house went out to join him.

Knowing what life could be like in an accident and emergency department, Polly wasn't unduly worried when the time crept round to quarter past and then half past eight, but when nine o'clock came and went without so much as a phone call she didn't know what to think.

Could she have mistaken the day?

In the confusion of her surprise at the invitation and his pager distracting the two of them, had he actually said eight o'clock—and had it been tonight or tomorrow?

Polly went over it carefully in her mind and was certain that he'd said he hoped to finish at eight tonight. That meant that he must have been delayed by some medical emergency.

Should she phone the hospital. . .? She toyed with the idea briefly, thinking that she could ask if there had been any major problems this evening—but how could she ask without drawing attention to the fact that it was Nick's whereabouts she was interested in? Wouldn't the hospital grapevine have a field day with that item of gossip? Sister Polly Lang chasing after Nicholas Prince!

She kicked off her smart court shoes and curled her legs under her in the big squashy chair in the corner by the window, resting her chin on her fist so that she could watch the comings and goings in the street with a steadily sinking heart.

For just a little while she had been ready to abandon her self-imposed restriction on getting involved. For just a little while she had almost let herself believe that something good could grow from the meeting of wounded souls which she'd believed had happened last night.

'Ha!' she laughed, a brief, bitter sound in the silence of the room. How could she have been so stupid as to allow herself to be fooled again? She knew only too well that men couldn't be trusted to keep their word, and she only had herself to blame for letting her guard down.

Even so, it was after eleven o'clock before Polly finally gave up her vigil.

She scooped up her discarded shoes in one hand and forced herself to walk calmly into her bedroom and push the door to, before stripping off her finery.

Force of habit made her hang her clothes up neatly but she found herself putting them away at the very back of the wardrobe. In spite of the fact that it was one of her favourites, she doubted that she would be wearing *that* outfit again in a hurry. . .

It was hard to remove her careful make-up without meeting her own eyes in the mirror but somehow she managed it, afraid of what she might see if she looked too closely.

Finally she was curled up under the covers, shivering slightly in spite of the warmth and comfort of her duvet and refusing to remember her half-formed expectation that by now she might have been sharing her bed with Nick. It took a long time, but eventually she fell asleep and was able to block out the leaden emptiness that filled the aching space around her heart.

As Polly approached the entrance portico of St Augustine's the next morning she was aware that, in spite of the drizzly rain, there was more than a touch of eagerness in her step and she cursed herself silently.

Although she would never admit the fact to a living soul, she'd been badly hurt by the fact that yesterday had been the first time since her divorce that she'd taken a chance and agreed to go out for a meal—and Nick had stood her up without so much as an explanation.

Still, she couldn't help hoping that there was a simple reason why he hadn't arrived last night, and as soon as she reached the department her eyes were scanning the various white-coated members of staff, hoping to see a familiar set of broad shoulders.

Unfortunately, the first time she saw him he was moving too quickly to notice anything around him, dashing across the corridor to disappear through a set of double doors into one of the major trauma rooms.

She peered briefly through the wired glass safety window as she hurried past on her own errand, but the bright lights were shining down on a badly injured patient, surrounded by a forest of equipment, and at least five or six frantically busy medical staff. The only way she could tell which of them was Nick was by the

colour of his hair, the blond strands shining like plati-
num under the lights.

Within minutes an ambulance arrived from one of
the large farms in the area where hunter trials were in
progress, and Polly dived in at the deep end with no
chance to think about anything but the job in hand.

'This is Olivia Harper,' began Ted Larrabee, his face
shining with sweat induced by the combination of the
warmth of the hospital, hard physical exertion and having to wear the waterproof layer of his paramedic's
uniform. 'She's eighteen, and her horse hit a jump and
fell on her. It was several minutes before we could get
her out from underneath. Her pelvis is very painful.'

'Lord. . .' Polly murmured, her eyes taking in the
slender blonde's pale sweaty face under the clear plastic
of the Entonox mask as she reached automatically for
the girl's wrist.

As she'd expected, the pulse rate was too fast and
Olivia's rapid breathing wasn't just the result of agita-
tion. 'What have you done so far?'

'One of the local GPs was on duty and, between us,
we managed to get two large-bore IVs up and running
with saline. She's had a small dose of ketamine to help
her cope with the journey, but we only waited long
enough to put a collar on her and strap her on the
full-length backboard before we rushed her here. She's
tachycardic but her blood pressure's still normal.'

He handed Polly his notations of their patient's vital
signs and she added it to the clipboard which was the
start of her casenotes. She noted mentally that the combination of readings Ted had given her meant that so
far Olivia was unlikely to have lost much more than
ten per cent of her blood volume.

There was no room for complacency, though, because

apart from minor abrasions there was no obvious sign of a bleeding wound, and she'd seen similar situations change for the worse in the blink of an eye, especially if, as she suspected, the patient was haemorrhaging internally.

'Olivia? Can you hear me?' Staying well out of the way of the member of staff who was cutting away a very expensive-looking set of riding clothes, Polly leant over and carefully tucked two fingers into one pale, cold hand. 'Can you squeeze my fingers?' There was a weak but definite increase in pressure on her fingers and Polly smiled.

'Good girl,' she praised, relieved that the youngster was aware enough to follow directions. 'My name is Polly and I'm a nurse, Olivia. You've had an accident and in a minute we're going to move you off the stretcher and onto a bed. I want you to let us do all the work. Do you understand?'

There was another squeeze but when Polly received the signal from Leo that they were ready for the transfer and tried to take her fingers away she met with resistance, and glanced down to find a pair of hazel eyes looking up at her pleadingly.

'Please. . .' The whisper was so weak that Polly almost had to lip-read it.

'What is it?' She leant closer and lifted the edge of the mask slightly. 'What's the matter?'

'My horse. . . Jessie. . . Is she. . .?' The hazel eyes filled with anguished tears.

'I don't know, sweetheart, but I'll try to find out,' she promised with a sympathetic smile and an extra gentle squeeze of the pale fingers.

For several minutes there was very little conversation, other than brief orders and requests from Leo, while the various items of mobile life-support and monitoring equipment were disconnected and Olivia was hooked up to the hospital system.

Polly had her back to the door when the ambulance crew called out their farewells so she wasn't aware that the set of footsteps behind her had any special significance.

'Have the bloods gone up?' a deep voice demanded and her heart leapt alarmingly as she realised that Nick had just entered the room.

'Yes, and she's gone on O negative while we're waiting for group and cross-match,' Leo confirmed. 'We've got plenty of plasma and expander ready to go in case her pressure starts dropping. I've also sent a message to Alex Marshall on Orthopaedics. By the time he gets here we'll have the X-ray plates developed. Apart from anything else, she's badly bruised.'

Nick nodded briefly, his face expressionless as he looked straight past Polly to ask one of the other nurses to pass him Olivia's notes.

Polly knew that an emergency room was hardly the time or place for personal conversations, but over the next few minutes she gradually became aware that, far from being carefully discreet about their new intimacy while they were surrounded by colleagues, Nick was actually looking straight through her as if he'd never seen her before, his grey eyes as cold as permafrost.

CHAPTER FIVE

'I DON'T like the look of this,' Polly heard Leo mutter in an aside to Nick. 'Just the slightest pressure on her pelvic bones causes pain, and they look uneven enough *without* an X-ray for confirmation of at least one break.'

'I agree,' Nick said decisively. 'We can't do any more down here without the X-rays because we don't know if we're dealing with spinal injuries or not and, meanwhile, she could be bleeding out. Let's get her ready to go straight up to Theatre. Her pictures can join her there, rather than doing a detour down here. Get hold of Alex and tell him about the change of plan. . .'

'Her blood pressure's dropping,' Polly broke in hurriedly. 'Not very much yet but she's losing ground, and in spite of everything we're pumping into her she's not responding to—'

'Right, that's it! Move it, people. . . We don't want to lose her,' Nick said sharply, cutting right across Polly's words, and the team was galvanised into furious activity.

Within seconds Olivia had been switched from the piped oxygen supply to a mobile unit, and the portable monitoring equipment was stacked across the end of the trolley for the rapid transition up to Theatre.

'Doors,' Leo called as the side rails clanged up into position and the wheels were unlocked. With the minimum of effort the bed began to glide swiftly across the room. 'We don't know what damage has been done internally so we don't want to jar her any more than we can help.'

Polly was closest to the double doors and gave a practised flick so that first one and then the other slotted back onto their automatic catches.

'Ready,' she called as she preceded the entourage out into the corridor to make certain there were no obstructions on the way to the lift. She knew from long practice that it could make quite a difference to the transit time if she went ahead to press the call button so that those doors could be ready and waiting, too.

As soon as they were safely on their way up she returned towards the emergency room, suddenly realising that she might have a chance to speak to Nick now that his part in the drama was over.

She was so preoccupied with her thoughts as she turned the corner that it took several seconds for her to realise that it was Nick's figure she could see striding away from her towards the opposite end of the department.

'Nick!' Polly called as she hurried after him, almost having to run to catch up as his long legs ate up the distance. 'Dr Prince, wait. . .'

She rounded the next corner in his wake and nearly ran into him as he stood, facing her, in the middle of the corridor.

'Sorry. I didn't expect you to stop just there. . .' she began breathlessly, but the words congealed on her tongue when she saw the anger in his gaze and wondered if calling after him had been terribly indiscreet. She'd never contemplated having a liaison with a colleague—even a fledgling one such as the relationship between Nick and herself—and had no idea of the proprieties.

'Well?' he barked. 'What did you want?'

'N-Nick?' She was almost speechless with shock at his harsh tone. What on earth gave him the right to be so rude? It wasn't as if *she* was the one who had stood him up last night.

'Come on. I haven't got time to waste,' he prompted. 'Why did you come chasing after me?'

'Well, an apology wouldn't go amiss,' she retorted and closed her mouth tightly, her teeth almost grinding together as she seethed.

'Apology accepted,' he snapped coldly. 'Perhaps you'd do better to. . .'

'What do you mean, "apology accepted"?' she demanded, so utterly incensed that it was difficult to remember to keep her voice down. 'I'm waiting for an apology from *you*—or is a consultant above the normal rules of polite behaviour?'

She glared defiantly at him, so angry at his high-handed attitude that she barely noticed his startled reaction to her accusation.

'The last *I* heard,' she continued forcefully, denying him the chance to interrupt, 'good manners dictate that you turn up on time when you've made arrangements to meet someone, and if you're going to be late you do your best to send a message. And as for standing someone up. . .!'

She didn't bother finishing the sentence, letting the disgust in her voice carry the message.

'A lesson from Miss Manners?' he taunted bitterly as he folded his arms across his chest and stared down his nose at her. 'And where in those rules for good manners and polite behaviour does it tell you how to deal with someone who doesn't bother to tell you that she's not free to accept your invitation?'

'Not free?'

Polly didn't understand what he meant. It wasn't as if she was still a married woman. . . He knew she was divorced, so what was he talking about?

After the heartbreak of that time she'd made a decision not to get involved again, and since then she'd hardly even spoken to a man on a personal basis, let alone. . . But he couldn't know about that, nor could he know that just one night in his arms had even tempered her fear of being hurt—her fear of taking a chance and trying again.

'*Doesn't* she look puzzled and innocent?' he derided with a sneer on his face. 'Perhaps you should learn to be a little more discreet when you arrange your meetings. Your social calendar seems to be a little full at the moment.'

'What. . .?' Polly had no idea what he was talking about—she didn't *have* a social calendar because she didn't have a social life.

'Still,' he continued, ignoring her confusion, 'you can cross me off your list as a one-night stand.'

Polly gasped in shock, her face flaming at his cruelly unfeeling reference to their night together. Had the soul-searing magic she'd been so certain they'd shared been so unimportant to him that he could belittle it like that? Had *she* meant so little that he could deliberately hurt her like this?

Well, she thought, drawing in a steadying breath and straightening her shoulders, she'd be damned if she was going to let him know how deep the wounds went. A sudden bitter inspiration struck her and she stared straight into his wintry grey eyes to deliver her parting shot.

'Don't worry, Dr Prince, you can be certain that it

won't be happening again. Usually, you kiss a frog, hoping it will turn into a prince. Unfortunately, I had the bad luck to do it the other way round!'

She turned smartly on her heel and strode firmly away, determined that Nicholas Prince would *never* know how much he had hurt her.

For the rest of her shift Polly threw herself into her work with a vengeance, but even though her hands were seldom unoccupied she still found her thoughts circling back to the unanswered question. Like a pebble in a shoe or a thorn in a finger, it wouldn't let her forget it.

Why?

Why had he reacted like that when, just one short day ago, he had smiled at her and asked her out for a meal—even stolen a hasty kiss in the middle of the corridor?

Why had he said those hurtful things?

It was almost as if. . .as if he hated her or, at the very least, didn't have any respect for her.

Even through the difficulty of trying to calm a young woman in the pain and heartbreak of an ectopic pregnancy she found herself trying to work out what she had done to change his attitude towards her.

It wasn't until she was finally lying in bed, staring up at the pale nothingness of the ceiling, that she realised what she was doing to herself—realised how self-destructive she was being.

'Stop it!' she said aloud, her voice echoing back sharply from the pastel peach walls like a deliberate order.

'You've been through this scenario before,' she continued in a slightly quieter tone, mindful of the other tenants in the building but still determined that she wasn't going to travel down the same devastating road again. 'You keep making the same old mistakes—trying to take the blame for every situation on your own shoulders. This time break the mould and take another look—see whether it really *is* your fault.'

Systematically, step by step, she went over the events of the last few days.

The first significant step seemed to have been her decision to speak to Nicholas Prince about his over-harsh criticism and erratic mood swings when he was on duty.

She'd been under no obligation to tell him that she wasn't going to stand by and watch him demoralise her nurses, she reminded herself, but her well-developed sense of fair play had prompted her to speak.

She had never dreamt that the self-contained man she thought she'd known would have told her such details about his private life, and her sympathetic heart had gone out to him when she'd found out about the traumatic loss of his wife and child and the impending anniversary of the event.

It had been the fault of that same compassionate heart that she had wanted to see him the next night, worried about how he was coping with the devastating memories and his own misplaced feelings of guilt, but when Sister MacDonald had specifically asked her to deliver his wallet—giving her a cast-iron reason for being there—the decision had been taken out of her hands.

If she hadn't looked in through his window and mis-interpreted an innocent scene into a suicide attempt she liked to think that she would probably just have completed her errand and gone home. As it was, she'd spent the evening learning about a completely hidden side of the enigmatic man as he'd shown her around his house, and they'd ended up sharing his magnificent hand-made bed.

'But I don't understand,' she whispered into the darkness in a voice choked by suppressed tears. 'If he was so insistent that we needed to talk that he asked me to go out for a meal with him why didn't he turn up? And why does he seem to be blaming *me*?'

The lack of answers was frustrating, but at least she had now sorted through her memories and was certain that, as far as she knew, she wasn't to blame for his change of mind.

If only . . . the small voice in her head said wistfully, and she smiled up at the ceiling. Those two words had to be the saddest in the whole language and she seemed to have spent so much of her life saying them.

If only Andrew hadn't died. If only Tim had been more patient. If only. . . If only she'd stuck to her guns and stayed well clear of any entanglements.

Still, while there was no remedy for the events of the past she could certainly avoid similar pitfalls in the future. All she had to do now was contrive to stay out of Nick's way as much as possible and, with any luck, they would eventually be able to work together as if none of this had happened.

Perhaps, one day she might even know *what* had happened.

As she curled up on her side and clutched a spare pillow in her arms honesty forced her to admit that dispelling her own mistaken feelings of guilt wasn't making her feel any happier but at least, now that she'd put her thoughts in order, she would hopefully be able to relax enough to go to sleep.

She had another full shift to work in the morning, and she would need all the sleep she could get to make

sure that she could cope with whatever the day—and
Nicholas Prince—chose to throw at her.

Her only real consolation was the memory of his
shocked expression when she'd all but called him a
frog. . .

'Sister.' Leo's voice hailed her as she passed the door
and Polly detoured immediately, a smile already on
her face.

Over the last week or so the good-looking young
registrar had obviously noticed the chilly atmosphere
between Polly and Nick and seemed to have set himself
up as her champion, deliberately asking her to work
beside him on numerous occasions. It was just unfortu-
nate that in a growing number of cases the patient's
condition had necessitated calling in Nicholas Prince
as well.

Polly stifled a resigned sigh when she saw that this
time her nemesis was already in the room, his tall frame
bent forward in concentration over a young patient who
couldn't have been more than five years old.

'Fell into a cold-frame,' Leo muttered. 'Legs and
arms cut to blazes—full of glass and bleeding like a
stuck pig—but at least it didn't touch her face.'

The next half-hour was a torment as she fetched and
carried to order, monitoring their small patient and
responding as promptly to Leo's smiling requests as to
Nick's growled orders as they battled to stop the poor
child from bleeding to death.

Finally, they had little Emma stabilised well enough
to transfer her up to Theatre.

'Did you put in that request for extra supplies of
blood?' Nick demanded brusquely as he stripped his

bloodstained gloves off with a snap and pulled his mask down to hang around his neck.

'Yes, sir.' Polly's reply was coolness itself. 'Mr MacFadden is scrubbed and waiting, and Dr Panagiotis is on his way to set up for the plastic surgery.'

He grunted a reply but Polly was already turning towards Leo as he came back from his trip upstairs, the porter following him with the trolley.

'Does he think he'll be able to save her leg? Will she be able to walk?' she demanded eagerly, still horrified by the depth and extent of the damage done by the enormous shards of glass embedded in the child's flesh.

'No guarantees—it'll depend how much of the muscle he has to take away. Some of that glass in there looks as if someone's emptied a sugar bowl into the wound and given it a stir so it could be hours before she's off the table.'

Polly winced at the graphic description but she knew what he meant and what a problem it was going to be for Ross MacFadden. He would have to continue the job they'd started of irrigating the wound to remove as much of the glass as he could and then excise what couldn't be washed away in case it worked its lethal way into other structures of the body.

She sighed silently and turned to finish putting a fresh disposable cover on the bed and checking the supplies they'd used. She knew that her part in the child's recovery was over. Now it would depend partly on the surgeon's skill and partly on luck exactly how much muscle had to be taken away.

That, and how much permanent damage had been done to the nerves and tendons, would decide whether little Emma would be able to run and play again, or even if she would be able to walk.

The next patient through the door almost seemed like light relief after Emma.

'Which one's the doctor?' said a hoarse voice as a burly man came to a halt in the doorway, his eyes flicking from one member of the group to another. Tina Wadland looked quite tiny beside him as she tried to usher him into the room, but he was refusing to move, one large hand padded in a fluorescent pink wadded-up towel and cradled gingerly in the other.

'If you'd like to take a seat on the edge of the bed, Mr Percheron,' Tina prompted, and Polly had to turn away to hide a smile. She caught sight of Leo's expression and nearly laughed aloud—the name was so wonderfully apt! His muscular body even seemed to resemble the big heavy horses. . .

'Not till I know who's the doctor,' he said warily, looking from Leo to Nick and back again.

'Both of us,' said Nick, taking charge of the situation in a voice as smooth as silk. 'Come and tell us exactly what's wrong. Are you in pain?'

Mr Percheron nodded, his face pale and sweaty. Polly had the feeling that the big man was probably feeling faint and didn't really want the task of trying to lift a young Goliath off the floor.

'Can I help you?' she offered with a calm smile. 'If you're in a lot of pain you'll probably want to sit down.' She was careful not to jar his hand, creating a comfort zone around him with an outstretched arm as she directed him onto the table.

Out of the corner of her eye she saw Nick approaching and had to concentrate on what she was doing.

'Do you want me to unwrap the towel or would you rather do it yourself?' Polly offered him the choice so that he would be forced to take the initiative, otherwise the stand-off could last for ever.

'I'll do it myself,' he said, hurriedly moving it out of her reach and treating her to the same suspicious glare as the rest of them. Slowly he unwound the bright pink cloth, drawing in a hissing breath through his gritted teeth when he accidentally jarred it.

There were several seconds of silence when his hand was revealed, one finger sticking up at a most peculiar angle.

Polly made the mistake of looking towards Leo. Just one glimpse of the sparkle in his golden eyes was enough to have her fighting a fit of the giggles again. From the big man's reaction, they had expected at least a partial amputation or a spectacular puncture wound. A simple dislocation seemed such an anticlimax.

'May I have a look, Mr Percheron?' Nick requested, as he approached their apprehensive patient.

'What are you going to do with it? Will you have to cut it off? Only I can't stand this pain, but. . .but I don't like needles neither.'

'Well, then.' Polly watched the consultant smile reassuringly at the big man and her stomach clenched. He'd smiled at her, too, before. . . She dragged her attention back as Nick continued speaking, his deep voice infinitely calm and reassuring. 'If I could just have a closer look at it to see what we need to do?'

Polly watched Nick pointedly fold his arms before he leant forward to look at the painful digit and wondered why—until she saw the way Mr Percheron relaxed when he realised that no one was going to be touching it. Yet.

Nick made quite a pantomime of looking all round

the finger from every possible angle, then frowned thoughtfully.

'I'm going to need to touch your finger to see how badly you've damaged it,' he said, fixing Mr Percheron with a serious look. 'I'll be as quick and gentle as I can, but I'll need to squeeze your finger and I need to feel the back of your hand.'

Mr Percheron went a shade paler at the thought.

'And if I let you do that you'll be able to tell me what's wrong with my finger?'

'I promise.'

It seemed as if all of them were holding their breaths while they waited for the answer.

'OK,' the big man agreed hoarsely, and presented his hand on the outstretched palm of the other—like some delicacy being offered to a diner in a restaurant.

It was only then that Nick unfolded his arms and took a step closer. In a smooth action, which showed exactly how many dozens of times he'd had to perform the same manoeuvre, he gripped the meaty hand in one of his, the upraised digit in the other and gave a steady pull.

'Ouch! Dammit. . .!'

Mr Percheron's outraged shout coincided with the audible click as his dislocated finger slid back into position.

Nick released his hold and stepped back swiftly— almost as if he was taking the precaution of removing himself from the range of those meaty-looking fists.

'How does that feel?' he queried. 'Can you move it?'

His attention having been instantly distracted from glowering threateningly at the man who'd caused him pain to his precious finger, the big man concentrated on gingerly bending the finger and straightening it again.

'Hey! It's working again!' he exclaimed in disbelief. 'I thought I'd broken it right off.'

'No. You'd only dislocated it, and the quicker we got it back in the right place the less the likelihood of permanent damage,' Nick explained, then gestured towards Polly. 'Sister will tape it for you to give it some support. . .'

She tuned out the rest of his explanations, knowing that they were only for the benefit of the patient. She'd taken care of so many like it that she could almost do the work blindfolded. The thing she couldn't cope with was the fact that Nick hadn't so much as looked at her when he'd consigned the patient to her care, and he'd left the room immediately after.

'It always surprises me,' Polly commented when Mr Percheron had disappeared out of the room far faster than he'd come in. 'He's such a big man, but he was almost shaking in his shoes at the thought of what was going to happen in here.'

'That's the point, though, isn't it?' Leo said pensively. 'It was the *thought* of what we might do that was terrifying, and that makes him no different from the rest of us. We've all got things which frighten us— some real and some imagined.'

'In his case, pain and needles,' she agreed.

'And in yours?' Leo questioned for the first time, his voice quiet and his eyes full of concern. 'You haven't been looking very happy lately.'

'Perhaps I'm just afraid of having doors slammed in my face,' she said cryptically.

'Perhaps overcoming your fear depends on how badly you want what's on the other side of the door,' he suggested, all traces of the facile charmer gone. 'It would be a shame if you let something precious slip away because you're afraid of opening a door. . .'

Polly stared at him in the growing silence and saw the serious side which he usually kept so well hidden, and for the first time she realised that perhaps he hadn't just skated easily through life on a joke and a smile.

'I'm sorry.' The teasing expression was back in force as he raised his hands in a gesture of surrender. 'I'll stop practising psychology until I'm qualified.'

'I think you probably *are* qualified, but you make certain nobody knows you've taken the practical route,' she said quietly, feeling her way instinctively. 'The only way you could speak like that is if you've been through something like it yourself.'

'Who, me?' he started to scoff, then closed his lips tightly and drew in a deep breath. '*Touché*,' he murmured, and saluted her with one finger in imitation of a fencer's gesture.

'Bad?' she questioned sympathetically.

'Bad enough.' He closed his eyes briefly, but she'd already seen the pain.

She gave him the second he needed to push it aside, knowing that he wasn't one to talk about the shadows in his life either.

'Still, what can't be cured must be endured,' he said in a resigned tone. 'Unlike you,' he continued with a touch of determination. 'Up until a couple of weeks ago you seemed to be perfectly happy in your work and well able to keep the likes of us rabble in line if we tried to step too close.'

He raised one eyebrow like a question mark but she just shrugged, not knowing what to say. She hadn't told anyone at St Augustine's about the circumstances which had resulted in her return to full-time nursing and her

application for the job in A and E, and now was not
the time to start. After the pain of her brutal rejection
by Nicholas Prince her emotions were far too close to
the surface.

'Well,' he conceded gracefully, 'my shoulders are
broad if you ever feel you want to use them, or,' he
added as if he'd just thought of it, 'if I seem a little too
callow and lightweight you could always talk to Nick.
He's good at—'

'No!' She was aghast at the thought of confiding her
troubles to the man who now seemed to be at the centre
of them. 'I couldn't! He. . .he doesn't even *like* me. . .'

'*That* can't be true,' Leo declared instantly, seeming
quite taken aback. 'He thinks you're a damned
good nurse.'

A swift glow of pleasure suffused her face but she
fought to ignore it, knowing that Leo's eyes were
mercilessly sharp.

'You wouldn't know it, the way he snaps and growls
at me,' she pointed out, trying to hide her hurt.

'You can't tell me he frightens you,' Leo said dismissively. 'I didn't think *anything* frightened you—
and, anyway, I thought you knew his bark is worse than
his bite.'

The heat in Polly's cheeks increased as she
remembered Nick biting her, and just how gently he
had done so. . .

'No,' she said, her voice slightly breathless as she
tried to banish the memory, while remembering the
thread of the conversation they were having. 'It's not
so much people that frighten me as— Hey! What about
you?' she demanded suddenly, needing to turn the tables
on him before her distracted state had her spilling her
every thought. 'I've been hearing rumours.'

'Rumours about what?' he demanded warily. 'Anyway, I thought you didn't listen to rumours.'

'Ah, but this was such a juicy one. . .about you and Sexy Samantha up on Obs and Gobs?' Polly taunted, having heard about that young woman's determined pursuit of Leo Stirling.

'That's not a rumour, that's a *nightmare*,' he retorted with a theatrical shudder. 'That barracuda scares the living daylights out of me. Have you seen the upholstery on her? If I bumped into her in the corridor I could suffocate before anyone rescued me!'

Polly burst out laughing.

'You don't mean to tell me that you won't be taking her to the Ball? I would have thought a playboy like you would have jumped at the chance.'

'No way!' He looked over his shoulder with a haunted expression. 'Can you remember how much of her overflowed that skimpy strapless thing last year? I'm just glad I've got a cast-iron excuse not to take *anyone* this year. I'll be fully occupied with the Auction.'

'Speaking of which,' Polly said, finally letting him off the hook as they both began to make their way back towards the reception area, 'how's the new idea working? Did the people who made the promises go for the comedy idea? I've hardly had a chance to speak to you since you wined me and dined me in such style under the trees the other day so I haven't heard the latest update.'

Before Leo had a chance to answer a sudden noise in the doorway they were just passing drew their attention and they came face to face with Nicholas Prince, an arrested expression on his face.

'Problem, Nick?' Leo said. 'Anything I can help you with?'

'No.' He sounded preoccupied, and Polly noticed the way his eyes were going from Leo to herself. 'No problem,' he confirmed, and turned away from them.

Polly didn't have the heart to restart the conversation with Leo. She didn't think she would have been able to concentrate on anything he said.

All she could think about was the strange expression on Nick's face when he'd looked from Leo to herself, and when she recalled that they'd been talking about their meeting on the lawn to discuss the auction she had a sudden mental image of the white-coated figure she'd seen through the window.

Could it have been Nick, watching them? Was that why he'd made the comments about her busy social life—or was she clutching at straws in an effort to find a reason for his anger towards her?

Her heart ached when she remembered how tired Nick had looked—so grey and drawn.

She had hoped that once the anniversary of his wife's death had passed he would have returned to his previously inscrutable self, and had looked forward to some sort of respite—at least until the rawness of his accusations had subsided.

Unfortunately, he seemed to be working longer hours than ever and, in spite of the fact that she had tried to harden her heart towards him, she was now seriously worried that he was headed for some sort of breakdown.

'Does he *ever* go home?' she demanded in a fierce undertone as she swung to face Leo. 'He's absolutely exhausted and it's not good.'

Leo took her by the elbow and ushered her into the nearby staffroom, glancing around to check that their conversation couldn't be overheard before he turned to face her.

'Not good for the department, or not good for Nick?' he challenged perceptively.

'For. . .for both, of course,' she hedged, unable to meet his eyes as she felt the blood rush to her cheeks. 'That's why the new rota system was put into operation—so that there was always a senior person on duty, not so that the same person was on duty all the time!'

'You obviously care about him, and you know better than most that an experienced nurse like you can do an awful lot to lighten the load. . . Yet you seem to be doing everything you can to stay out of his way.'

'I *have* been working with him,' Polly protested heatedly, stung by the suggestion that she hadn't been pulling her weight and only just remembering in time to keep her voice down. 'Sometimes it feels as if the two of us spend the whole day joined at the hip. . .!'

She bit her tongue to stop the flood of words but from the expression in Leo's eyes she could see that it was already too late. She'd already revealed how difficult it was for her to work so closely with Nick.

'Ah, Polly,' he murmured and shook his head.

She hated the glimpse of pity in the dark gold of his eyes, and suddenly she couldn't bear the thought that he might have guessed what had happened between Nick and herself; couldn't bear that he might have guessed how much she had come to care for their irascible boss and how little it mattered to Nick; couldn't bear that Leo might be feeling sorry for her because her feelings weren't returned.

'Don't you worry about me, Leo Stirling,' she

declared huskily, her chin coming up and her shoulders straightening with determination. 'I'm a survivor, and I've got the scars to prove it.'

CHAPTER SIX

'DAMMIT, Leo! Don't you dare do this to me again!'
Polly snarled. 'You've been pushing me into Nick's
pocket for days and it's. . .it's utterly childish!'

She didn't dare mention the fact that Leo's campaign
to keep Nick and herself in close proximity was the
most excruciating mixture of pleasure and pain that
she'd ever experienced. He would probably see that as
some sort of success and redouble his efforts to effect
some sort of understanding between the two of them.

She might as well have saved her breath because all
she got in return for her objections was a shrug from a
broad pair of shoulders and a wave as Leo disappeared
into the lift with the patient he'd volunteered to take
up to Theatre.

It wouldn't have been so bad if she hadn't caught
the broad smile which crept over his face just before
the doors slid shut.

'I've been set up—again!' she muttered, as she
turned back towards the emergency room and her next
stint as the other half of Siamese twins. 'Can't he see
that it isn't doing either of us any good?'

She glanced across at Nick but he seemed supremely
indifferent to Leo's manoeuvres. It was Hannah's
puzzled frown she encountered as she turned to the task
of setting the room to rights.

All she could do now was hope that the rest of the
day was particularly quiet so that she could spend as

little time as possible in Nick's presence. Anything else didn't bear thinking about.

Unfortunately, it didn't look as if she was going to get her wish because within a matter of minutes she was answering a call from the ambulance control station.

'Priority. Major incident,' the voice said, and her heart sank as she recognised the code and reached for her pen.

Soon she was scribbling as fast as she could go, pausing only to beckon to Hannah as she underlined the words 'mobile medical team'.

Hannah nodded and took off at a fast walk, leaving Polly to take down the rest of the details—her hand flying towards the computer terminal in between to call up essential information onto the screen.

By the time she'd finished with the call there was already an extra buzz in the department, which told her that Hannah had passed on the message, and she grabbed the clipboard and went to join the fray.

She was looking down at her notes as she left the room or she'd have seen Nick coming in the other direction. As it was, they struck each other a glancing blow and she reeled back against the wall.

'Polly! I'm sorry. . .' He grabbed her flailing arm to steady her and she was suddenly aware of the warmth of his hand on the soft flesh of her arm. 'Are you all right? You should watch where you're going. . .'

'I'm sorry, sir.' She pulled away from his hand, angry with herself that she was reluctant to break the contact when he seemed totally unaware of it. 'I was checking my notes,' she continued, concentrating on the important matters in hand.

'Sister Nicholls said they need a mobile medical team so I've paged Leo. Now, what have you got?' He turned

to follow her back into the office and perched one hip
on the corner of the desk, the casual pose completely
belied by the intensity in his face.

'A car apparently out of control in the town centre
has mown down pedestrians. So far the estimates of the
number of casualties reported range from several to
dozens, but Ambulance Control will clarify as soon as
possible. God only knows what the severity of the injuries will be or what type but, as you know from Hannah,
they asked for a mobile team.'

Nick nodded, his brow furrowed with the intensity
of his thoughts. 'I don't know who the other nurse on
duty is, but Leo and Hannah are getting kitted up and
John Preece is on his way down.' Polly recognised the
name of the anaesthetist and could picture his lean wiry
frame and quicksilver wit.

'We'll probably have the first of the walking
wounded arriving in a few minutes so can you start
clearing our department and Outpatients of all but the
urgent cases?' Nick continued briskly. 'As soon as we
get a more accurate picture of the numbers involved we
can make decisions about whether convalescent patients
will have to be discharged but, in the meantime, can
you organise a quick audit of the hospital bed state?'

'The audit's already under way, via the computer. . .'
Polly gestured over her shoulder towards the omnipres-
ent electronic equipment '. . .and a message has gone
out to the operating theatres that routine admissions
have been cancelled and cold surgery deferred until
further notice. They've been alerted to make ready for
casualties, and so have Radiography and Blood
Transfusion, and extra staff have been mobilised.'

'Good.' He blinked as if amazed by how much she
had achieved already.

Polly pointed towards the computer again. 'The wonders of technology—all that phoning and running around achieved at the touch of a few buttons.'

'If only treating patients could be as easy,' she heard him mutter under his breath, then his head came up as he recognised the significance of the sudden increase in noise. 'That sounds like the first of them arriving. Let me know as soon as we get some figures so I can decide whether to call in any more staff. . .' As he was speaking, he'd straightened up from his desk and was striding out of the room.

For a while Polly was in charge of the control centre, with responsibility for the mobilisation of the various levels of personnel. When the number of reported casualties reached the twenties, with more arriving under their own steam—as well as those being ferried by ambulance—the department was beginning to groan under the sheer weight of numbers.

The sound of distressed humanity was becoming quite deafening, especially when the relatives and friends of the injured started arriving to demand information.

In spite of her experience with such situations, faint glimmers of panic were winding their way through Polly when a group of determined pressmen and -women tried to invade the department. She could have hugged Celia MacDonald when her superior bustled into view, every inch of her uniform immaculate in spite of the fact that she was supposed to be off duty today.

'Right, everybody,' she called, her Scottish accent cutting through the hubbub effortlessly. 'If the media personnel would kindly follow that gentleman there. . .' she pointed to one of the porters '. . .he will show you to the room where the consultant will give you a statement.'

She paused just long enough for the eager group to get out of the way before she continued in an aside to Polly, 'Though when the consultant will have time to speak to you lot is another matter altogether!'

Polly chuckled.

'I'm glad to see you, Sister. I was beginning to think they were after my blood.'

'No problem. It all comes with experience,' she said lightly. 'Now, I recognise these two.' She indicated two well-dressed ladies, walking briskly towards her. 'They're the counsellor and the lady who organises the volunteers. They'll need the two little interview rooms, but if you'd like to get yourself off to the busy end of the department I think you're needed there.'

Polly agreed with alacrity, glad to relinquish the reins into the senior sister's capable hands.

On the way towards the reception area Polly had time to reflect on the enormous amount of organisation inherent in her job—and the fact that it would get worse when she eventually made senior sister.

Still, she consoled herself, Big Mac had a few more years to go before she retired so that meant there was plenty of time for Polly to learn all the finer points and practise them until they became second nature to her. After all, she, too, was intending to stay in the profession long term. There was no chance that she would be leaving to become a housewife—not a second time.

There was only time for the thought to be accompanied by an emphatic shake of her head and then she was in the thick of it; close to the ambulance entry.

The noise was much greater here, with the cries of the injured mixing with the sobs of those in shock and more than a few terrified children.

Over all, though, was the determined attempt at organisation, with triage being repeated for every patient as they came into the accident and emergency department.

'Sister.' Nick's distinctive voice reached her clearly over the din and she made her way straight across to him, the colour of his hair standing out like a beacon to guide her.

'Will you take over here with me while Sister Ohlen helps in Outpatients with the walking casualties?'

Polly nodded, but her agreement wasn't necessary—she would work wherever he told her to.

They were starting to see some of the more seriously injured casualties now, those who had been too seriously injured to do anything but wait for medical assistance at the scene.

As each one arrived Nick checked them over, making his own judgement as to whether they should be classified as immediate, urgent or non-urgent, and colour-tagging them accordingly with special labels.

To the uninitiated it might look like a waste of time to repeat the examination and tests done at the scene of the accident, but she knew that out in the field it could be all too easy to miss tiny vital clues—such as the tell-tale area of bruising which could herald a massive internal bleed.

When Nick was satisfied with his decision the casualties requiring immediate care were sent to resuscitation areas, urgent casualties to the main treatment areas and the non-urgent cases were directed to the outpatient department where the minor treatment area had been set up.

Polly always found this one of the most frustrating

aspects of a major trauma. She knew that the triage work was essential so that the team could provide the greatest good for the greatest number, and she was as meticulous as ever in incorporating the information on the notes begun at the site of the accident into the hospital records. But she would rather have been working in either the resuscitation area or one of the main treatment areas where she would have been actively nursing.

'Hello, Polly,' a familiar voice greeted her, albeit in a subdued tone, and there was Leo. 'Last live casualty,' he reported formally, then continued in the familiar shorthand. 'Flail chest. Don't know if he'll make it—they had to cut him out of the car with the jaws—and he's high as a kite on something. . .'

Polly realised suddenly that this patient was the cause of all the misery she'd been seeing for the last hour but, although she knew that Nick would have made the same connection, it made no difference to his professionalism as he began to check him over, the two of them setting off at a brisk trot towards the resuscitation area with the trolley between them.

As this was the last live patient to leave the scene John Preece had travelled back in the same ambulance and followed close behind.

'No seat belt on,' Leo continued, while the monitoring and life-support systems were transferred over, 'so when he finally smacked the big concrete planter at the base of the tree his ribs didn't stand an earthly against the steering-wheel. Both femurs gone,' he detailed as he pointed out the injuries to the patient's legs. 'One of them's been pushed right up through the socket, by the looks of it, so his hip's probably a mess—to say nothing of probable internal injuries. And, on top of that, he hit his head on the door pillar and knocked himself out and there's a query on a neck injury.'

'Blood pressure's terrible,' Polly interrupted. 'He must be losing an awful lot of it somewhere, in spite of two large-bore IVs running in flat out.'

She glanced up in time to see Nick and Leo look at each other in concern.

'Lung?'

'Spleen?'

The suggestions were simultaneous but the result was the same, with John Preece ensconced behind his high-tech equipment to monitor the anaesthetic while the two of them began work on opposite sides of the body.

There was a brief pause while X-rays were taken and quiet relief when there was no evidence of a neck injury, but the rest was done with dogged determination as they found and stabilised one injury after another.

'It's still too low,' John said into the desperate silence. 'If we can't. . .'

He was interrupted by the shocking single tone which told them that their patient's heart had stopped beating.

'Dammit! No!' Nick shouted in frustration. 'Don't you dare. . .!'

They worked on him for the next ten minutes, first with chemical stimulants and finally—because they daren't put any pressure on his broken ribs in case they punctured his lungs—they tried open-heart massage and direct electrical stimulation.

'Nick?' Leo questioned, one eyebrow raised when there was still no viable response.

'OK,' he conceded, his voice weary as he straightened up and stepped back from the trolley, his hands dark with blood. His eyes flicked up towards the large clock-face on the wall. 'Note the time of death,' he added flatly, before he stripped off his gloves and apron and strode out through the doors without looking back.

Worried about the strangely dead expression she had seen in his eyes as he'd turned away from the body, Polly wished that she could go after him. She knew that he must be reliving the death of his wife and longed to comfort him, but there was work to be done.

She stepped forward to begin detaching the ECG leads but Leo's hand halted her.

'Go with him,' he murmured quietly. 'We can manage here.'

'But. . .' She looked up at him, for a moment thinking that this was just another episode when he tried to push the two of them together, but his expression told her that Leo knew about Deanne, too.

'What good can I do? He doesn't even *like* me,' she reminded him in a hoarse whisper, wishing that it wasn't true—wishing that she had the right to go and offer him comfort.

'But he *needs* you.' Leo's simple words were as solemn as his expression so she couldn't doubt him.

With a tentative half-smile she nodded and turned away to strip off her own disposables and hurry after Nick.

'Which way did Dr Prince go?' she demanded when she nearly cannoned into Tina in the corridor.

'Towards Reception,' the young woman said, then grinned cheekily. 'And he didn't even growl at me. . .!'

Her humour fell on deaf ears as Polly took off in the same direction, guessing what she would find.

'Sister MacDonald.' She greeted her superior with a smile. 'How is the staff rotation going? Have we got enough relief in for Dr Prince to take a break?'

The blue-grey eyes examined her intently for a

second. 'Lost him, did we?' she said astutely, and Polly knew that it wasn't really a question.

She nodded and her eyes were drawn across to the tall figure, speaking to the uniformed policeman—no doubt filling him in on the fate of their culprit.

'In which case, I think a break might be a good idea—for both of you. The rest of the "immediate" patients have all been dealt with and have left the department, and the "urgent" ones are well in hand. There's nothing here that can't wait an extra fifteen minutes while you both catch your breath.'

'Thank you, Sister.' Polly gave a rather wan smile. 'Now all I've got to do is persuade him to do it—what do you suggest? Shall I throw him over my shoulder?'

'Go on with you, lassie!' The usually stern face softened into a broad smile. 'He'll go if *I* tell him to!' Polly watched with bated breath as the diminutive woman bustled swiftly across the department and spoke to the burly policeman, before turning her attention on the tall man standing tensely beside him.

'What did you do?' Nick demanded with a tired display of aggression when he followed her into the room two short minutes later. 'Did you bribe her to make me take a break?'

Polly glanced up at him warily as he stood just inside the doorway with his clenched fists held rigidly against his sides and his jaw set, then she turned away just long enough to carefully put down the two empty mugs she was holding in case the temptation to throw them at him grew too much to bear.

'I thought about it,' she retorted as she turned to face him with all the calm she could muster. 'But in the end she didn't think she'd need danger money because she noticed that you weren't wearing your Superman outfit, and she has no trouble dealing with mere mortals.'

It was definitely a day for bad jokes, she thought as his grim expression remained unchanged, and she turned back to spoon coffee granules into the mugs and pour water over them from the steaming kettle. She had decided that she was going to stay calm and make allowances for his bad mood, especially after the way he had reacted to the loss of their patient, and the sheer domesticity of the commonplace actions was soothing.

'Here,' she offered as she carried the brimming mugs over and put them on the low table, proud of the steadiness of her hands. 'Black. No sugar.' She sank into one corner of the four-seater settee and leant her head back against the soft upholstery, grateful for the chance to sit down.

The silence stretched out between them but Polly was determined not to let it upset her. They had both needed a break and she'd made certain that they'd got one. That was all there was to it. . .

'Thank you. . .'

For a minute she didn't move, thinking that she'd imagined the husky words.

'Polly?'

Slowly she allowed her eyes to open, hardly daring to believe that he wasn't sniping at her.

In spite of his size she hadn't heard him move, but now he was sitting on the chair set at right angles to her own, his elbows planted on his knees and the coffee-mug clasped between his long-fingered hands like a lifeline while he stared down into its dark depths.

Slowly he raised his head, his stormy grey eyes lifting to meet hers, and as she watched he dropped an opaque veil over the emotions revealed there until once more she was seeing the calm enigmatic persona he presented to the world.

'I needed this,' he admitted quietly, gesturing with the mug before he took the first mouthful.

Polly found herself watching his every movement as though mesmerised, her eyes charting the way the harsh artificial light bleached the blondest streaks in his hair to silver and painted shadows in the tired hollows under his cheek-bones.

She already knew that his eyelashes were several shades darker than his hair, but she hadn't really noticed before quite how long and thick they were. On a less virile man they could have seemed almost feminine, but on Nick they just accentuated the. . .

'Polly?'

She blinked when his voice interrupted her self-indulgent train of thought, then leant forward swiftly to pick up her own steaming mug, hoping against hope that he hadn't noticed the way she'd been gazing at him.

'I'm sorry,' he murmured into the silence, the quiet words jerking her eyes up from their contemplation of her own mug to see him gesture towards the patient they had just lost. 'I didn't cope with that one very well and I had no right to take it out on you like that, especially when you were only using your common sense.'

'Well. . .' She paused for a minute, the unexpectedness of the admission leaving her almost speechless.

It was true that his reaction to the young man's death had been extreme but, even so, he should have known better than to carry on without a break—especially when he'd made certain that there were enough members of staff to cope.

There was no way she was going to mention the fact

that Leo had said that his boss *needed* Polly's company. But still. . .

'You'd certainly have torn Leo off a strip if he hadn't taken a break when it was time to,' she pointed out as gently as she could, and held her breath, not knowing if she had pushed too far.

'True,' he admitted with a heavy sigh. 'I don't know why this one hit me the way it did—God knows I've dealt with plenty of them since Dee. . .

He glanced up at her and, in spite of the fact that they hadn't even begun to talk about the rift between them, their gazes caught in wordless communication for several long seconds before he looked back down at his mug with a wry smile. 'Perhaps it's a good thing we've got our resident Scottish dragon breathing fire down our necks to keep us in line. . .'

Polly felt the smile creep over her face and chuckled as she visualised Celia MacDonald as a dragon—a very small dragon to face down Nicholas Prince in one of his towering tempers. . .!

'Sister? Do you know where. . .? Oh. . .!' Tina Wadland subsided in confusion when she came flying into the room and found the intimidating consultant, who had reduced her to tears, laughing aloud.

Polly saw the speculative look that crossed the junior nurse's face as her eyes went from Nick's smiling face to her own and she groaned silently.

For days Nick had been cold and cutting towards almost everyone in the department and now, within minutes of going off for a break in her company, he was apparently in high good humour. Just wait until the hospital grapevine got hold of *this*.

'Yes, Tina?' Polly prompted, with a mental shrug of resignation.

'Oh.' The young woman gulped audibly and Polly watched the tide of colour sweep over her cheeks as she met Nick's direct grey gaze, then dragged her eyes away hurriedly as she delivered her message. 'Sister MacDonald asked me to apologise for disturbing your break, Doctor, but could you go to her office as soon as you're free?'

'No peace for the wicked,' he groaned with a wry smile for Polly, and she had to swallow another chuckle when she saw the stunned expression still decorating Tina's face as she hurried out of the room.

'What?' Nick demanded, and she realised that she hadn't been as successful as she'd hoped at hiding her amusement.

'Nothing much.' She dismissed his question with an airy wave of her hand as she watched him drag himself unwillingly out of the depths of his chair and tug his white coat straight. 'Just that there's one young nurse who will never be quite as frightened of you again.'

'What?' he repeated, clearly at a loss.

'She's found out that Old Nick knows how to laugh,' Polly explained wickedly. 'Just wait until she spreads *that* rumour around!'

The sound of his groan of disgust stayed with her for hours as she went about her duties, her heart lighter than it had been for days.

Still, at the back of her mind was the unsolved puzzle as to why Nick had treated her the way he had. Why, after spending the night together in his magnificent bed and then arranging to take her out for a meal the following evening, he had apparently decided not to bother to turn up.

Worse still had been the way he had cut her dead the next time they'd met at the hospital, and the hurtful words he had used like weapons when she had tried to confront him.

She shrugged, wondering if she would ever find out what had happened to change his mind, but when she contemplated asking him for an explanation she found herself silently shaking her head. Much as she wanted to know the answers, they weren't as important as the fragile truce which seemed to be in force between them.

Luckily for her proccupied state of mind, the department was fairly quiet for several hours—almost uncannily quiet—so that the call that came through from Ambulance Control just half an hour before she was due to go off duty came almost as a shock.

'Triple car pile-up. Three injured on their way in. One with multiple injuries and smoke inhalation, one with a possible neck injury and one with thirty per cent burns and smoke inhalation.'

Polly swore silently, knowing how devastating such injuries could be, and hurried to pass on the information, but it wasn't until the first ambulance arrived that she realised that the burns victim was a young child who had been trapped in her safety seat when the car she'd been in had burst into flames after the crash.

'Gently!' she reproved sharply through her mask as their tiny patient was transferred as rapidly as possible onto the hospital's life-support and monitoring systems.

The injured little body was swathed in sterile water-gel dressings, but in spite of the fact that she was covered by a blanket to prevent systemic heat loss the poor child was shivering uncontrollably, her eyes tightly closed above the smallest size Entonox mask.

Swiftly checking the plasma and saline drips already set up and running, Polly completed the task of drawing off blood samples for cross-matching and testing for haemoglobin, electrolytes and urea and sent them straight up to the lab. Then she joined in the awful task of removing the rest of the poor mite's clothing.

'All right, Fiona,' she crooned softly as she worked. 'It's all right, my sweetheart. We're looking after you now. . .' She kept up her low-voiced litany, never certain just how much her little charge could hear or understand, but knowing instinctively that if she *was* listening she needed to hear something more than the usual impersonal medical conversation which surrounded such an injury.

For a brief moment, when the full extent of the little girl's injuries were uncovered, she met the wintry grey of Nick's eyes above his mask and she knew that they shared the same thoughts.

Each recognised that this amount of damage was going to mean months of hospital treatment while grafts were harvested from the uninjured regions of the child's body to cover the large areas of full-thickness burns. They could only guess at the amount of pain she was going to suffer while the treatment continued.

A little wordless moan from the child between them drew their eyes down again and, after a swift demand for a further dose of morphine, it was Nick who bent forward to speak gently to her.

Polly saw him administer the drug as soon as it was handed to him, then watched as one lean hand ventured up indecisively before he stroked the sweat-soaked hair behind a soot-blackened ear.

'Hang on, Fiona,' he murmured softly, his deep voice full of caring as he tried to calm her. 'The pain will soon be gone, sweetheart. . .'

In that second Polly knew that she had fallen in love, but not with the disguise Nicholas Prince hid behind—

the persona of a big, self-contained man who fought against allowing anyone to come too close although, heaven knew, even like *that* he drew her like a magnet.

No, the man she loved was the gentle, loving person who lived inside the mask—the man who recognised that a tiny child needed more from him than just his medical expertise and who didn't care who saw him comforting her.

CHAPTER SEVEN

IT WAS sheer will-power that helped Polly to keep her mind on the job as the team eventually managed to stabilise little Fiona enough for the journey to the specialist burns unit. The fact that she had just made such a momentous discovery about her feelings for Nick couldn't be allowed to detract from her care of the suffering child.

Unfortunately, she seemed to have used up her day's quota of self-control on the job because, when Nick threw her a quick smile of appreciation for team work well done, she couldn't help the way her eyes followed him when he finally left the room.

Even when the doors had swung closed behind him she continued to stare blankly in his wake, stunned by the changes which had come over her in such a short time. It had been years since her husband had let her down badly, and she'd sworn then that she would never let another man turn her life inside out. She hadn't even been tempted until. . .

'Aha,' came a gleeful murmur in her ear and she jumped, blinking as she turned to find Leo grinning down at her.

Her frantic hope that the preoccupied expression on her face hadn't betrayed her vanished when she saw the way his golden eyes were gleaming with unholy mirth.

Her heart sank as she fought the heat rising up in her cheeks.

'You've got it bad, haven't you, Polly, girl?' He

sounded as if he was taunting her, but underneath the glee there was an air of. . . Was it delight? Whatever it was, Polly was too flustered to care.

'I—I don't know what you mean,' she stammered weakly, feeling the heat envelop her neck and face in spite of her efforts as she turned quickly away from his knowing gaze.

Her eyes flicked rapidly around the room, partly because she was worried that his words might be overheard by the other members of staff still in the vicinity, but also because she didn't dare take a chance that he might guess the true nature of her recent discovery.

She drew in a steadying breath before she turned to face him again. It was bad enough that he thought she was attracted to their boss—she had listened to his brand of teasing often enough and dreaded being the butt of it—but if he realised that she'd fallen in love with Nick. . .

'Perfect!' Leo crowed under his breath as he rubbed his hands together. 'Just a few weeks ago the two of you hardly noticed each other, in spite of the fact that you've been working together practically joined at the hip, and now. . .!' His laughter was full of open delight, and several pairs of eyes turned their way.

'Leo. . . Please. . .' Polly implored when she saw the attention they were attracting.

'Come on, then,' he urged, grabbing her by the elbow and barely allowing her enough time to get rid of her disposables before he dragged her out into the corridor. 'Perhaps I could start a secondary career as a matchmaker. Wait till I catch up with Nick. . .'

'No!' Polly squeaked, the soles of her shoes protesting on the shiny surface of the corridor when she refused to move an inch further. 'Don't you dare!'

She was horrified by the turn of the conversation. Her brain was already whirling with the confirmation that Leo had been deliberately throwing her into Nick's path, but for him to make a joke about the fact that his tactics had resulted in her falling for Nick. . .

'If you dare to say *anything* to him I'll. . .' She cast about frantically for a threat terrible enough to guarantee his silence, then found the perfect one. 'I'll tell Sexy Samantha that you'd be delighted to escort her to the Autumn Ball!'

'Oh, no! Not that!' he protested, and Polly was amazed that he seemed genuinely alarmed by the prospect. 'Please, Poll, promise me you won't do that. I couldn't stand another evening of fending her off, especially as I'll have my hands full trying to organise the auction. You couldn't be so cruel!'

'What's he whinging about now?'

Hannah's question cut through the intense confrontation, and for the first time Polly witnessed the way Leo's naked discomfort was quickly hidden behind his usual thousand-watt smile and the teasing glint in his eyes.

'I was just offering to find him a partner for the Autumn Ball,' Polly said, responding to the silent appeal he threw her way. Well, in a way she was only telling the truth. . .

'Since when has *he* needed someone to drum up partners?' Hannah scoffed. 'The last time I looked they were taking numbers and standing in line.'

'How well organised! And which number are you?' Leo challenged flirtatiously.

'Oh, I'm far too discriminating for that,' Hannah retorted with a grin for Polly. 'I want to know that I'm the *only* one on the list before I'll agree to go out with a man!'

Polly glanced up at Leo and realised from the quick narrowing of his eyes that he, too, had seen the shadows hiding behind Hannah's cheeky bravado.

'Obviously not a match made in heaven, then,' she quipped lightly, breaking into the suddenly prickly silence. 'On the one hand we have a man reputed to have a host of followers, and on the other a lady who doesn't like to be one of the crowd. It seems as if the two of you are destined to be nothing more than friends.'

'If that!' Hannah retorted tartly and briefly flicked her eyes to the watch pinned to the front of her dark blue uniform. 'Still, at least we can rely on him to provide the entertainment for the Ball—either intentionally or accidentally—when his harem closes in for the kill!'

Polly watched as her friend swept off down the corridor with her head in the air, and she couldn't help the chuckle of approval which escaped her.

'Hey! Whose side are you on?' Leo demanded.

'I pride myself on not taking sides,' she retorted primly, trying vainly to subdue a smile, 'but, after your admission that you've been sticking your nose where it wasn't wanted, I'm thinking of making an exception. . .so watch your step!'

'All right! All right!' He backed away from her, both hands raised in submission. 'If you'll promise not to involve your pneumatic colleague, I promise not to try to push you and Nick together. . .in spite of the fact that I think the two of you would be—'

'Leo! Enough!' she cried in exasperation. 'Get back to work before I make that call up to Obstetrics!'

He subsided, grumbling under his breath about

ingratitude as he returned to Reception.

The rest of Polly's shift was relatively quiet, filled with a complete mixture of the sort of minor ills and ailments which should never have been brought to an accident and emergency department in the first place.

'When will they ever realise that they're supposed to go to their GP for this sort of thing?' Hannah muttered as she cleared away the debris from a session of syringing out an elderly gentleman's ears. '*And* he had the nerve to complain that he'd been kept waiting for twenty minutes.'

'He's lucky he came when we weren't rushed off our feet with a *real* emergency or he wouldn't have been seen at all—just told to make an appointment with his GP's practice nurse to have it done,' Polly commented as she removed the paper sheet covering the trolley and unrolled another length. 'Some days I reckon anything up to three-quarters of the people sitting out there, complaining about the amount of time they're kept waiting, shouldn't even be here at all.'

'*You* know it, and *I* know it, but how do we get *them* to realise that they're wasting everyone's time when they clog the system up unnecessarily. . .? Oh, what's the use of telling you?' Hannah pulled a face. 'You know it as well as I do.'

'I think everyone in the department has ridden *that* hobbyhorse at some time,' Polly agreed wryly. 'But until Mr and Mrs A. N. Other out there get the message we're wasting our energy getting cross about it.'

'True,' Hannah agreed as she reached for a fresh set of disposable gloves. 'At least Reception now tells them that if they're non-urgent cases there might be a long delay. The prospect of an indefinite wait does persuade a few of them to take their problems elsewhere.'

The room once more returned to pristine readiness, the two of them left to collect their next charges.

Although she wasn't working with him the whole time Polly had time to notice, during the rest of her shift, that Leo seemed unusually subdued.

He worked quietly beside her while they took care of stitching up a rather nasty gashed arm where a youngster had slipped while climbing between several rows of barbed wire, and he complimented her on her quiet proficiency as she calmed a young child and held him still while Leo retrieved the lentils the youngster had pushed up his nose.

On her way home Polly congratulated herself that her threat to deliver Leo into the hands of his nemesis seemed to have worked.

It wasn't until he wasn't doing it any more that she realised exactly how often in the last few days Leo had stepped aside with his thousand-watt grin to allow Nick to work beside her.

Not for anything would she admit, even to herself, that she was actually missing the chance to work so closely with Nick. She had the greatest respect for him as a doctor, which was only increased by the depth of her emotional attachment to him, and although she hadn't realised at first that it had been a deliberate ploy on Leo's behalf she had enjoyed the chance to spend so much of her time at Nick's side.

Still, she sighed as she finally stretched her tired muscles and curled up under the puffy duvet, she would be seeing him again tomorrow and the day after that, and her empty soul would have to be satisfied with that.

After the heartbreak she had suffered five years ago she had made a decision to avoid any permanent relationships, and she knew from what he had told her about the tragic end of his own marriage that Nick's past had left him too raw to be looking for anything more than friendship. . .

As she drifted into exhausted slumber she tried to ignore the numb grey ache that surrounded her heart but, for the first time, she couldn't subdue an unaccustomed feeling of regret which followed her into her dreams.

'Polly. . .I need you,' Leo called cheerfully, and beckoned to her just before he disappeared around the corner.

'Oh, but. . .' Polly closed her eyes in exasperation at yet another summons, then turned back to make her apologies to Nick—again. 'Excuse me. I'd better see what he wants.'

As she turned away she saw the swift scowl which drew Nick's brows together over his steely grey eyes and realised just how often she'd seen it happen over the last few days.

Mind you, she thought as she set off in pursuit, it was hardly surprising that Nick should be getting more than a little annoyed with the way Leo was carrying on.

The trouble was that it seemed as if it was all her own fault.

Ever since she'd told Leo to stop matchmaking and had threatened him with a fate worse than death— the prospect of an evening in the company of Sexy Samantha—he'd turned the tables on her completely. Instead of engineering situations so that she and Nick were almost constantly working together, whenever he saw her anywhere in Nick's vicinity now he seemed to find another task which needed her urgent attention.

Unfortunately, several other members of staff had

seen what was going on and, although they didn't know *why* he was doing it, they thought it hilarious, especially when he began peppering his conversation with flowery words and phrases and fulsome praise.

Her blood came close to boiling point when she thought about how many times he'd called her *sweetheart* and *darling*, and the way he put his arm around her waist and squeezed as he gazed down at her with his big golden eyes.

Why? she railed silently. Why was it that she was the only one who could see the laughter hidden there as she was powerless to curb his nonsense? And why was it that when he did it she was never quick enough to retaliate—to tread on his toes or jab him in the ribs with an elbow?

It hadn't taken her long to realise that Leo's changed tactics were an attempt at making Nick jealous. She might even have been able to see the humour in the situation if it wasn't for the fact that the truce between Nick and herself was so new and frail that instead of drawing them together Leo's activities were driving them further apart.

Unfortunately, the realisation of just how much Nick had come to mean to her was still fresh and untried. She'd barely had time to wonder if, in spite of her fears, there might be a chance of some sort of relationship between them when Leo had begun his campaign of disruption.

There was no chance of that now, with Nick glaring at whichever one of them happened to be nearest— his temper slowly fraying at the edges as the whole department began to join in.

It didn't matter that Polly had tried several times to have a quiet word with him to explain what was really going on. Somehow, each time she made a move Leo seemed to guess what she intended to do and managed to head her off with another over-the-top display of flattery and appreciation until Nick was well out of the way.

She'd even tried to corner Leo to plead with him to stop his nonsense, but he'd only taken advantage of the situation when Nick chose to walk past at the same time.

'Nick! Help!' he called in mock fear as he wove his fingers firmly between Polly's and raised their joined hands to the wall above his head. 'Get this woman away from me!'

Too startled by his antics to think about struggling against his hold, Polly's horrified eyes watched as Nick approached. His stride barely altered as his eyes flicked coldly over the two of them before he continued word-lessly on his way.

'Leo!' Polly implored under her breath, her cheeks flaming as she realised what their little tableau must have looked like to the disdainful consultant passing by. To anyone who hadn't seen the way her fingers were trapped between Leo's it must have seemed as though it was *Polly* who had him pinned helplessly in position. 'Let me go, you idiot!' she demanded. 'This isn't funny.'

There was an audible catch in her voice and the pressure behind her eyes warned that she was close to tears so when he finally released her she whirled away and fled to the nearest bathroom to lock herself in. Too bad if someone else needed the toilets—they would just have to go to the other end of the unit.

She leant her head back against the door and drew in several deep, slow breaths while she fought for control.

In the plain oblong mirror she could see the way her

hands were curled into white-knuckled fists and the tension in her face was evidence of the way her teeth were clenched tightly.

Fixing her eyes on the image in the mirror, she concentrated on relaxing her jaw and allowing the muscles in her hands to release their tight grip.

Gradually, she realised that it was not despair that was tying her up in knots but a deep, complex anger.

There was anger towards Leo for playing his silly games, however well-meant; anger towards Nick for taking Leo's play acting at face value and judging her accordingly, but most of all anger at herself for allowing the situation to get to her as badly as it had without either calling a halt to it or retaliating.

Not that she would ever do anything which would jeopardise the work of the department—God forbid that the patients should suffer—but the more she thought about it the more she realised that it was time Leo swallowed a little of his own medicine.

'Polly? Are you all right?'

The tentative words were accompanied by a quiet tapping on the door behind her head, and she smiled wryly. Since she'd moved to St Augustine's Hannah had become the best friend she'd ever had. It created a warm glow in the cold corners of her heart to know that there was someone who genuinely cared about her and wouldn't hesitate to come to her defence.

'I'm fine, Hannah,' she murmured just loud enough to carry to her friend. 'I'll be out in a minute.'

She straightened up and walked towards the hand basins, determination squaring her shoulders as she went.

'Are you really all right? What happened?'

Polly smiled easily when she found Hannah waiting

for her as she emerged from the bathroom.

'I'm fine. Really,' she insisted, and knew that she meant it. Those few minutes had been enough to get her feet firmly on the ground again.

'But what happened? Tina said there was some sort of a fight in the corridor.'

Polly chuckled aloud. Trust the hospital grapevine to get the whole story mixed up!

'Nothing happened, Hannah,' she reassured her friend, giving her arm a squeeze. 'I just needed a quick breather and the only place to be alone in this place is the loo!'

'Are you certain? Only I know Leo has been a pain in the backside the last couple of days and Old Nick has started breathing fire and brimstone again so it could have been either of them—'

'Hannah, I'm OK. Honestly. In fact, I'm better than OK so let's get our sleeves up and get on with the job.'

Polly led the way towards Reception with a fresh spring in her step. Just let Leo try any of his silly tricks and he'd find out what Polly Lang was like when she went on the warpath!

'Polly, sweetheart, could you lend me a hand?' Leo said in his most cajoling tones, and Polly smiled to herself before she turned round. She hadn't thought that he would chance his arm quite so soon, but Nick had just walked into the room and it was obvious that Leo's campaign was still running.

What a shame he didn't know that the rules had changed. . . Still, he'd soon learn. . .

'Of course, Leo,' she said sweetly, pointedly rolling her eyes for the other people in the room.

Nick's face remained impassive, but Tina had to stifle

a giggle. Like the rest of the staff, she'd been following the byplay all day and fairly goggled as she watched Polly join Leo by the small kitchenette area where he was boiling the kettle to make some coffee.

'What can't you manage? Can't you find the sugar, or are the mugs too heavy for you?' she mocked, and was delighted to see the deep flush which swept over his face when he realised that she'd finally called his bluff.

John Preece had arrived a little early for his shift and had taken advantage of the time to relax bonelessly in one corner of the settee. He'd already made himself a mug of coffee and nearly drowned himself with it when he saw Leo's reaction.

'Uh, no,' Leo said uncertainly as he glanced over his shoulder towards the sight of Tina, thumping John's back while he fought for breath. 'I. . .er. . .wondered if you could help me pass the mugs round.'

'No problem,' Polly agreed easily as she reached for the two mugs already filled. 'I'll take these two for Nick and myself, shall I?'

Before Leo could comment she'd turned away with her hands full, delivering the first one to the coffee-table in front of a darkly frowning Nick.

'Shh!' she signalled with a finger to her lips and another exaggerated roll of her eyes towards Leo, hoping Nick would appreciate the way she had finally spiked Leo's guns.

For a second she was afraid that he wouldn't respond, but then she had the pleasure of seeing comprehension of her tactics dawn on Nick's face. Suddenly the eyes which had frozen her with their wintry chill had a sparkle like moonlight over rippling water, and one corner of his lips tilted briefly into a smile.

As she stepped away to find a chair he nodded

towards the empty seat beside him and raised one eyebrow.

'Thank you,' she murmured, feeling an unaccustomed shyness as she took up his silent invitation to join him.

She tried to leave a careful space between them but managed to nudge his shoulder as she subsided, and even when she murmured an apology and shuffled away to break the contact she could still feel the heat emanating from the long lean length of his thigh.

'Oh.' Leo's voice broke into their wordless communication and the two of them turned to gaze up at him silently as he stood there with his mug of coffee, neither of them making any effort to make room for him to join them.

'I'll. . .er. . .find another seat, then,' he mumbled, seeming unexpectedly uncomfortable with the situation, and Polly was hard pressed to fight down a giggle.

'One of these days you'll have to tell me what all that was about,' Nick murmured under cover of the renewed conversation in the room.

'When I work it all out myself I promise you'll be the first to know,' she retorted, hardly able to believe that all it had taken was one determined stand, in front of witnesses, to stop Leo in his tracks. And she'd wasted so much time trying to get him alone to talk some sense into him. . .

'So you and Leo aren't what they call an item?' Nick asked. His tone was apparently idle but his intent grey eyes weren't when he turned to meet her startled gaze.

'Hardly!' Polly scoffed and her heart began to thump unevenly when she realised that they had finally started talking to each other. Perhaps now she would have the chance to explain all his misconceptions, and ask for a few explanations herself.

She managed to keep her voice steady as she tried to decipher Nick's impassive face. 'He's not my cup of tea—or coffee!'

'I thought he was every nurse's ideal?' he prompted lightly. 'He's certainly never lacked for company ever since I've known him.'

Polly looked across at Leo and smiled to herself at the very idea that Leo could be her ideal.

She'd seen him watching Nick and herself for several seconds after he'd moved away from them, as though contemplating whether to make another attempt at joining them, but his attention had been caught by one of the other staff members and he'd soon ignored the two of them to perch himself on the arm of one of the chairs on the other side of the room.

Now he was apparently busy teasing Tina and making her blush.

'Oh, he's ideal if you don't mind taking a number and waiting in line,' she said, borrowing Hannah's assessment of the situation. 'I don't doubt that, one-to-one, he's a lot of fun to date, and he's intelligent and hard-working and I could write him a wonderful testimonial, but. . .' She shrugged, not bothering to finish.

Her frankness seemed to startle Nick but his laughter was overshadowed by the strident sound of the telephone. Leo was closest and he was still joking with Tina as he stretched across the back of her chair to grab the receiver.

As soon as he answered the call Polly knew from the way his expression changed that they weren't going to like what was coming in.

'RTA,' he announced in the familiar shorthand

almost before he'd put the phone down. 'We've got two policemen arriving in less than ten minutes. Someone rammed their patrol car and nearly came through the windscreen at them.'

There was a wordless murmur of anger in the room as they all reacted to the thought of yet another injury to vulnerable public servants. Polly had noticed, in the limited time of her own involvement in the specialty, how many more such injuries were turning up in Accident and Emergency departments.

It didn't seem so long ago that policemen, doctors and teachers were treated with the same respect and care as the elderly and the very young. Now it seemed as if no one was safe any more. . .

It wasn't until the two victims arrived that the team found out that one of them was a young female, only recently transferred to the area.

'Oh, God,' Tina whispered in horror when the young woman, wearing a neck brace and strapped to a back-board, was wheeled in under the unforgiving brightness of the lights. 'Her poor face. . .'

It wasn't the first time that Polly had seen the effects of a face full of windscreen glass, in spite of the fact that the wearing of seat belts was law.

This time, though, the victim *had* been belted in safely. The problem was that the driver of the stolen car they had boxed in had decided to reverse into them at high speed in an attempt to push the patrol car out of their way, and had actually mounted the bonnet and pushed the windscreen in at the two occupants.

'First things first,' Polly reminded her young colleague, consciously quoting one of Nick's favourite phrases to steady her. 'Her face looks bad, but we have

to find out what other injuries she has before that can
be dealt with.'

'I know, Sister,' Tina agreed quickly. 'ABC—airway, breathing and circulation, but I'm glad Dr Prince
can send for the plastic surgeon to have a look at her.
I'd hate to think that she was going to have to live
with. . . Oh, Lord,' she squeaked, her eyes riveted on
the second trolley being wheeled into the other side of
the room. 'What's happened to *him?*'

Polly glanced across quickly at the second officer
and for a moment all she could see was the frantic
activity as he was stripped of his remaining clothes by
one set of hands, while others worked over and around
them to attach monitors, IVs and breathing apparatus.

Suddenly one of the team moved aside and she saw
the man's face for the first time.

He, too, was covered with dozens of cuts, but the
most startling aspect of his injuries was the way that
one of his eyes was nearly bulging out of its socket.

'It could be several things,' she said, keeping her
voice down as she turned her attention back to their
own charge. 'Can you think of any?'

Tina thought for a moment, then suggested, 'Could
it be the result of a blow to the eye socket? If the
cheek-bone was shattered, it could be forcing the eye
out like that.'

'Could be. Anything else?'

'Fractured skull?' she offered as she automatically
fetched and carried to order.

'Is that a likely cause? Think about it—what would
be causing the bulging?' Polly prompted, her own hands
working independently of her conversation as she
helped to prepare the young WPC for the attention of
the plastic surgeon. The X-rays of her neck and back

had been cleared and she would soon be ready for trans-
port up to Theatre for the long job of piecing her face
back together.

'No, I suppose it's not very likely,' Tina conceded.
'The fractured skull wouldn't cause the eye to bulge
out like that unless there was bleeding behind the eye
socket. Then the pressure could force the eye forward.'

Polly caught Nick's eye across the width of the room
and she could tell that he was amused by the way
the younger woman was verbally sorting through the
options, but there was also a gleam of approval for the
way Polly had used the event as a teaching situation.

For Tina's sake she was glad that her own mask hid
her smile as they listened to the quick-witted young
woman sorting through the possibilities. It was one of
the best ways Polly knew for taking the newer recruits'
minds off some of the uglier sights they saw in an
accident and emergency department, and it was amazing
how much they learnt this way.

'What about bleeding going directly into the eye
socket?' Tina suggested, with a quick glance towards
the other side of the room to check on events over
there 'Or if the blood supply to the eye itself has been
damaged, or. . .? Oh, God!' she breathed and Polly
heard her swallow convulsively when she finally saw
the reason for the prominent eye. 'His eye socket is full
of *glass*. . .!'

The final count, at the end of a backbreaking stint
as Nick painstakingly retrieved every tiny sliver, was
seventeen pieces of glass—some of them nearly half
an inch across—which had been forced into the eye
socket by the force of the collision.

'Will his eye be all right or is he going to lose the
sight in it?' Tina asked when Nick finally straightened

up and groaned in relief, his fingers digging into the muscles in his lower back.

'As far as I can tell, there's no major damage to the eye itself,' he said as he pulled his mask down to hang around his neck, then added on a cautionary note, 'We'll have to wait for the swelling to go down before we know for certain, but it looks good so far.'

He glanced up at the clock on the wall and groaned again. 'Thank God for that—it's time to go home.'

He stripped off his disposables and dumped them in the bin as the patient was wheeled out through the swing doors and towards the lifts. He rotated his shoulders as if he needed to work the stiffness out of them, too.

Polly was seized with the mad urge to offer to mass-age the kinks out, but she knew that the whole department would hear about it in a nanosecond and she'd never be allowed to live it down.

As it was, she just had to imagine what it would be like to be granted permission to touch his body and bring him comfort, the way she had once before. . .

The trouble was that the more she thought about it the less likely she was to be able to sleep tonight.

CHAPTER EIGHT

'HEY, Polly! Hang on a minute!'

It was only because she recognised Hannah's voice that Polly bothered to slow down, her umbrella trying to turn itself inside out as the wind tugged at it.

'Hurry up, then, or we'll both be soaked! Get underneath this thing with me—it might keep a little bit of the rain off you!'

The two of them scurried towards the main entrance, their feet splashing through the rivulets of water which coursed between the fancy paving slabs in front of the big glass automatic doors.

'Ugh! I'm wringing wet right up to my knees,' Hannah complained bitterly as they made their way along the corridor towards the staff cloakroom. 'Good job I've got a towel and a spare pair of tights in my locker.'

'Still, it's always warm enough inside the hospital to dry off fairly quickly—too hot sometimes, especially when you come inside on a winter's day. I've got a feeling that's why everyone seems to get so many colds these days—going from freezing cold to too warm and back again.'

'You could be right,' Hannah returned in a muffled voice as she nearly disappeared inside her locker, trying to unearth the elusive packet of tights. 'This place is better than my first job after I qualified, though. I swear the boiler there was so old it had to have coal shovelled into it all day just to keep the radiators lukewarm!'

She gave a crow of victory and backed out of the locker with the missing packet held aloft. A pale blue envelope floated to the rain-spotted floor like the last of the autumn leaves.

'What on earth. . .?' she muttered as she stooped to retrieve it. 'Ah! I'd wondered where that had got to. . .' Ignoring the state of her clothes, she ripped the flap open and fished inside to withdraw several sheets of closely written paper.

Not wanting to appear nosy, Polly turned back to her own locker.

Quickly retrieving several pages of yesterday's newspaper which she'd never had time to read, she crumpled them up and stuffed them into the toes of her shoes. If she was lucky, it would absorb some of the moisture before she needed to put them back on at the end of her shift.

'Fantastic!'

Hannah's jubilant cry quite startled Polly and she turned to find her friend waving her letter and dancing a damp-footed jig.

'I take it that's good news,' she commented wryly when Hannah finally stood still.

'The best!' Hannah promised. 'Do you remember me talking about one of the nurses I trained with—Laura Kirkland?'

'Didn't you both start off specialising in paediatric nursing together?' Polly said with a frown of concentration, her memory jogged by the fact that they had both started off on the same career track as she had done.

'That's right. Then I decided to change to A and E, and when I got the job here it looked as if we were going to drift away from each other.'

'It happens a lot when you move from one hospital to another,' Polly agreed. 'You get so wrapped up in the new job and a different set of colleagues that you don't seem to have time to keep up the old friendships.'

'And it doesn't help if you lose letters before you've even opened them,' Hannah added with a flick at the pale blue sheets. 'Laura wrote this nearly a month ago to tell me that she changed direction shortly after I did and she's now working in A and E, too.'

'What a coincidence!' Polly smiled at Hannah's pleasure, conscious of a twinge of regret that she hadn't kept in touch with any of the group she'd trained with. She'd still maintained contact when she'd married, in spite of the fact that her priorities had changed, but after she'd lost. . .

'Ah, but you haven't heard the best of it,' Hannah gloated, breaking into Polly's painful introspection, then glanced briefly at the letter again as if to check her facts. 'She's coming here—to St Augustine's.'

'To visit you?'

'No! To work!' she clarified, then added with a flourish, 'Laura's the new member of staff we've been waiting for!'

There wasn't time for much more conversation if the two of them were going to be on time, but Hannah was almost bouncing with pleasure at the idea that her old friend was going to be joining the team.

'Hey! She'll be here in time for the fund-raiser!' Hannah exclaimed a little while later. 'I'll have to put her name down for a ticket to the Ball. Do you think I should get an escort lined up for her? After all, she won't know anybody. Do you think Leo would be willing?'

'He said he was probably going to be too busy with

the organisation on the night to take anyone, and he *has* got Sexy Samantha waiting in the wings if he changes his mind!' Polly informed her, and they both had to stifle their laughter. It seemed to be common knowledge that Leo turned pale and hid whenever the busty barracuda appeared.

'Speaking of the Ball,' Hannah continued later on when they met up for a cup of coffee, 'have you heard any more about the Auction? Someone told me there's a rumour going round that there's going to be a surprise draw of some sort.'

'In which case, you know more than I do,' Polly admitted. 'I know Leo had some problems with the fact that the prizes were much more lavish than he'd expected and he was afraid it would put people off bidding, but he solved that one some time ago.'

'Well, if this draw is going to billed as some sort of surprise, he probably won't tell us, but if he's trying to drum up interest. . .'

'Unfortunately, if he drums up too much interest it's going to be hell trying to sort out off-duty for everyone who wants to go,' Polly said glumly. 'There'll always be someone who gets the short end of the stick, no matter how hard we try.'

'And you can't always operate a first come, first served system either,' Hannah elaborated, 'or the same people would always put their names down for every do, and the ones who have to hold off until they've found a partner or a babysitter would miss out every time.'

'Then, of course, there's always the possibility that there'll be some sort of major accident that evening and that the people who get the chance to go will end up dashing in to work in their evening clothes.'

Hannah chuckled. 'Wouldn't the inevitable press photos look good! I can see the headlines now—*The Best-Dressed A and E in the country*!'

'It wouldn't do much good for the fund-raising part of the evening if Leo lost all his potential bidders.'

'Well, there's not a lot of point in worrying about it until or unless it happens. I've bought my ticket and I found a gorgeous dress in that nearly new shop in the little road just past the library. All I've got to do now is find a pair of shoes and a man!'

They returned to the department and the next stream of patients, but Polly's brain was working overtime as she realised that her own situation had changed.

She had decided that as she didn't have an escort she wouldn't bother buying a ticket to the Ball. She had quite resigned herself to feeling very magnanimous about letting someone else have the evening off to attend.

Now she realised that everything was different.

Since she and Nick were talking again she couldn't help the fact that a little shoot of hope had started growing. Perhaps, as Nick was going to the Ball, he might decide to ask her to accompany him.

Her musings were abruptly shattered as a young woman staggered into the department, carrying two young children.

'Please, Nurse, help me. . . My babies are sick. . .!'

Polly reached her side just in time to catch one child as he slid out of her grasp.

As Polly took his weight she could feel how hot and feverish he was, his skin strangely red and dry.

'Can you manage to carry your little girl? We just need to bring them through here and the doctor will see them.'

'Yes...but please hurry. I think they've been poisoned!'

Out of the corner of her eye Polly saw one of the junior nurses hurrying to help, and she shook her head.

'I can manage here for a minute. Get Dr Prince—as quick as you can!'

She continued on her way into one of the emergency rooms with the young boy in her arms and laid him on a trolley, quickly raising the sides into position in case he rolled over, then she turned and held out her hands for the little girl.

'What makes you think they've been poisoned?' she questioned as she laid the second child on the same trolley. It wasn't until she saw how alike they were that she realised that the two of them were probably fraternal twins, but there wasn't time to comment on the fact. She had important information to elicit before Nick arrived. 'Did you see them eating something? Did they get hold of some tablets?'

'No. It's this. . .' The mother reached into her pocket and drew out a handful of greenery just as Nick swept into the room.

'Hello. I'm Dr Prince. What have you got there?'

'I'm not sure, but I think it's deadly nightshade. The children found it in the garden and they were eating the berries.'

The poor woman was shaking from head to foot, as pale and sweaty as her children were hot and dry. She was obviously terrified as she watched Nick bend over first one and then the other little one. 'I didn't know it was there—we only moved into the house two days ago and the kids have never had a garden before. . .'

'Well, they've certainly got all the classic symptoms of belladonna poisoning, including dilated pupils and tachycardia. Sister, let's get IVs running.'

While Polly collected the equipment and set up one IV Nick combined questioning the mother with setting up the second one, and soon he was ready to begin infusing the antidote to belladonna.

'I'm going to begin with a quarter of the dose over five minutes for each of them, and repeat until we see a change. Have some atropine ready in case we have to reverse any side-effects.'

Polly found she was almost holding her breath as the first dose went into the IV for each of them and then, five minutes later, a second one.

She shared the mother's delight when, just as Nick was administering the third dose, the two children started visibly responding to the antidote.

'Oh, thank God!' she breathed faintly, seeming to grow even paler as relief struck her, and Polly had to catch her and deposit her on a chair before she fell over.

By the time the final dose had been slowly infused it was obvious that the two little ones were well on the way to recovery.

Nick straightened up after his final examination and smiled.

'I think they're going to be all right now, but I'd like to admit them to the children's ward overnight for observation.'

'Oh, Doctor, you don't think they'll go unconscious again, do you?' Their mother had just started regaining some colour, but at the mention of admitting her precious babies she went as white as a sheet again.

'Not for a minute,' he soothed. 'But I would like them to stay on the drip for the time being, and the antidote can have some side-effects of its own so we like to monitor it.'

'But. . .'

'We do have facilities for parents to stay with their children so you could stay with them if you want to,' Polly prompted, and received a shaky smile of gratitude.

'Oh, yes, please. I couldn't bear to go home to an empty house without them. My husband had to leave this morning to start his next shift on an oil platform. He'll be away for several weeks but I told him I could cope as long as he was here for the day we moved house.'

She covered her quivering mouth with equally shaky hands.

'Oh, God,' she breathed tearfully. 'He's hardly been gone for a day and I nearly let our babies die. . .!'

'Hey! None of that!' Polly scolded gently. 'They're perfectly normal, mischievous youngsters who thought they'd found something nice to eat. It happens!'

'But. . .'

'But as soon as you realised what had happened,' Polly continued, not allowing her to interrupt, 'you did everything right. You got them here as fast as possible, and you remembered to bring a sample of the berries they'd eaten so we could identify it and administer the right antidote first time.'

'It's very kind of you to say so, but I still shouldn't have let them. . .'

'She's right, you know.' It was Nick who interrupted her this time. 'You did everything you should, and I'm willing to bet that the first thing you do when you get home is scour the garden for anything else they might want to experiment on, and tell them in no uncertain terms that they mustn't eat anything without asking first.'

'You're not kidding!' she said with feeling,

responding to Nick's gentle humour and his confidence
in her as much as the reassurance he was giving her.
'Could you put a padlock on their mouths while we've
got them here so I won't have to worry about this
happening again?'

'I don't think you'll have this problem again,' Nick
said wryly. 'All you'll have to do is remind them what
happened when they ate the berries—there aren't many
children who'd want a second dose!'

He'd finally managed to coax a chuckle out of the
poor woman, and Polly had a feeling that she would be
able to cope with the rest of the episode more than
adequately—after all, she'd had the courage to move
house with two inquisitive youngsters under school age,
and with the minimum amount of help. She and her
children were obviously survivors. . .

If only she could say the same for herself, she thought
wryly as she took the first opportunity to hide herself
in the tiny kitchenette round the corner from the consultant's office.

The room was too small for a chair so she had to
lean back against the work surface, but it wasn't until
she cradled both hands around the steaming mug that
she realised that they were still trembling in the after-
math of the tension of the last hour and she was grateful
that she had the room to herself.

When she remembered how close those two precious
children had come to death she felt physically sick—
the same way she had for the last five years ever since
the tragedy which had turned her own life inside out.

Oh, it wasn't bad enough that she couldn't do what
had to be done—if anything, the tension inside her
seemed to make her hypersensitive to her little patients'
needs. But afterwards, even when the outcome was as

good as this one had been, she always felt totally
wrung out. . .

'Polly? Are you feeling all right?'

Nick's deep voice broke into her gloomy introspection and she looked up from her contemplation of the
rapidly cooling contents of her mug to meet the concern
in his grey eyes.

'No. Yes. I'm fine,' she assured him, plastering a
smile on her face.

'I don't think so,' he said quietly as he stepped into
the little room and propped himself against the front of
the tiny sink. 'I've started to know when something's
not right. What is it? A headache, or are you going to
be the first flu victim in the department this year?'

The light touch of his humour was just what she
needed to release the tension inside her, and she felt
the knots in her shoulders begin to unwind.

'Yes and no,' she said with a wry smile. 'It's not a
headache in the accepted sense, but it is for me.'

'Explain.'

Eyes which could be as icy as an arctic wind seemed
softer and warmer as he encouraged her to speak.

'It's the children,' she began, then pressed her lips
together as she tried to find the words which would
allow her to explain, without laying bare her soul. She
wasn't ready for that, even though it had happened five
years ago, and some days she didn't think she would
ever be ready. . .

'Those twin imps?' he questioned with a frown, referring to their most recent case. 'What's the problem?
They're going to make a total recovery and are probably
already starting to cause a riot up—'

'No. Not just them,' Polly interrupted. 'It's all the
children, especially the babies. That's why I changed

from Paediatrics. I couldn't stand it any more. . .the reminders of what could happen. . .what did happen. . .'

'A bad experience?'

She nodded wordlessly, trying desperately to stop the tears from gathering, but her memories—coupled with his gentleness—were stretching her control to the limit.

'Do you want to talk about it?' he offered softly as he leant towards her, one hand stretched out in invitation. 'We could go into my office if you don't want to be interrupted.'

She squeezed her eyes tight and shook her head, drawing in a deep breath before she chanced using her voice.

'No. . . I—I don't want to talk about it. Thank you for offering but I'll be all right.'

'You're sure?' He reached out and placed one warm hand over hers as it curved around the forgotten mug in her hand.

The contact seemed to reach deep inside her, the warmth travelling all the way into the cold dark corners around her heart, and she found herself struggling for control again.

'I. . .I'm sure,' she whispered as her eyes travelled from the lean dark fingers, cradling her own slender paler ones, up to the intent expression of concern on his face.

Suddenly the love she had been trying to hide from him escaped her shaky control and she dragged her gaze away from the lean planes of his face, afraid that if she wasn't careful it would blaze up at him like light from a beacon.

She remembered the day when he had told her about his wife. His anguish had made it very clear to her that he had loved Dee and wouldn't be interested in an affair, permanent or otherwise. Honesty made her admit that, in spite of the physical attraction which had flared between them, she had no reason to suppose that he'd changed his mind. There'd been nothing private between them since his stolen kiss in the corridor—not even a chance to talk.

At least now he knew that there was nothing between Leo and herself, but what would he do if he realised how much she had come to love *him*? He was a fair-minded man. Would he feel that he was being unfair to her that he couldn't return the emotion?

She was burningly conscious of the fact that his hand still rested over hers, and she could feel his eyes skimming her face as clearly as a physical caress.

Was it just wishful thinking on her part that there was a new closeness beginning between them? A sensitivity to each other's thoughts and feelings?

Not so long ago she had been firm in her decision not to allow anyone to touch her heart. Now everything had changed.

But had it only changed for her? When they finally had their talk would Nick insist that they kept to a purely professional association? If he couldn't return her love might he even hint that it would be more comfortable for both of them if she were to look for a job elsewhere?

How would she bear it—to go away, knowing that she would never see him again?

She couldn't. Not after the searing heartbreak she'd suffered when her marriage had shattered around her. . .

The only solution was to make certain that he never found out how much her feelings had changed towards him, and the best way was to make certain that they spent as little time as possible together.

Nervously clearing her throat, she hunted for a way to put some distance between them and turned slightly so that when she pulled her hand away from the contact with his it would look casual.

'I'll be fine,' she repeated, and straightened her shoulders, lifting her chin a notch without meeting his gaze. 'I'll be out as soon as I've finished my coffee.' She turned away, knowing that she wasn't ready to face him yet.

She held her breath for a moment but he didn't comment on her rather obvious ploy, and the next thing she heard was the sound of his footsteps, leaving the cramped room and receding along the corridor.

Polly was worried that her clumsy attempt at dismissing his attention might have soured her working relationship with Nick. As it was, he seemed a little preoccupied and several times she had felt as if he was watching her.

Elsewhere in the department a child was rushed in by her parents with suspected meningitis, but when it proved to be a minor unexpected food allergy Polly allowed herself to relax again.

It was frustrating to react to children's emergencies like this, but she consoled herself that it was usually only this bad immediately after a close call. Within a few hours and after a dozen or more other patients she would be coping as well as ever.

Until the next time, a little voice inside her head reminded her, and she grimaced, knowing she couldn't deny it.

The next person she had to take through to a cubicle was an elderly man who was complaining that his leg felt 'all wriggly'.

'Would you like me to help you to slip your trousers

off so we can have a look?' Polly suggested, breathing shallowly as a defence against the rather rank odour of his grubby clothes.

'I'm not taking my clothes off for a slip of a girl to see my privates!' he exclaimed in horrified tones. 'It's not proper!'

'It's all right, sir. I'm a nurse and it's part of my job,' Polly explained gently.

'Well, you shouldn't be doing a job that gets you looking at men's privates,' he retorted belligerently. 'You should be at home, looking after babies and keeping things nice for your husband.'

Tim had thought the same thing, although she hadn't known that when they'd married, and her insistence on returning to nursing had been the reason why he had been able to crucify her with guilt when disaster struck. . .

'But I'm not married,' she explained calmly, forcing herself to concentrate on the confrontation in front of her rather than the one she'd never been able to win.

'There you are, then,' he said, inexplicably triumphant. 'I never showed my privates to my wife in forty years of marriage, and I'm certainly not going to show them to a slip of a girl who can't even catch a man of her own.'

Halfway through his tirade Polly was conscious that they weren't alone in the cubicle any more and she turned to find Nick, standing impassively behind her.

'Right, Sister, what seems to be the problem here?' he said. His voice was imperturbable but she could see a fugitive gleam of humour in his eyes and knew that he had overheard at least part of the old man's complaint.

'Mr Ferguson is complaining that his leg feels all wriggly, and I was just asking him if he needed any help to take his trousers off,' she said, keeping her face straight with difficulty.

'Fine,' Nick said, obviously taking the initiative before their elderly patient could get started again. 'In that case, Mr Ferguson, perhaps you can answer a few questions for me while I just slip your things down. Sister, could you get a clipboard to write the answers down?'

'Certainly, Doctor.'

She smiled as she slipped out of the cubicle and grabbed the nearest clipboard, knowing that it was just a ploy to enable the old man to save face. She and Nick both knew that she'd already taken the clipboard with the start of his case notes into the cubicle with Mr Ferguson.

By the time she returned the elderly man was sitting bolt upright on the examining couch, his body covered from his waist to his grey knobbly knees with a plain blue cotton blanket.

When he heard her draw the curtain closed behind her he glared at her, looking as if he wished he could pull the blanket down to cover the rest of his legs, too.

It wasn't his angry expression or the fact that his lower legs were naked that caught her eye so much as the gaping wound down the front of one shin.

Compassion for the pain he must have suffered when the injury happened and concern that such a large wound covered by such unsanitary clothing might have become dangerously infected—even gangrenous— made her take a step forward.

It wasn't until she caught the bemused expression on Nick's face that she took a closer look, and realised that the wound was teeming with maggots.

'*That's* why your leg feels wriggly, Mr Ferguson,'

Nick said with admirable aplomb, for all the world as if it were a sight he saw every day. 'Now, we'll just get Sister to clean you off and put a dressing over the wound, and you can get dressed again.'

'But what about the wriggling?' he demanded querulously as he squinted short-sightedly down at his leg, obviously unable to understand what was causing his discomfort. 'Will the wriggling go away?'

'Sister will get rid of the wriggling for you as soon as she uses some special stuff on your leg,' Nick promised, evidently giving up all idea of explaining what had happened in favour of solving the problem as swiftly as possible.

Before the cantankerous old man could remember that he'd objected to her presence Polly was carefully irrigating the gash, catching the stream of water and its various water-borne inhabitants in a strategically placed bowl.

'The wound is beautifully clean,' she commented in a brief aside to Nick.

'Good. That means the maggots had just about finished their work. Without them, he'd probably have lost his lower leg to gangrene.'

'What are you two mumbling about? What's happening to my leg?' The fretful voice held a touch of fear this time.

'Nothing at all,' Nick reassured him with a smile. 'You've given it a bad knock at some stage, and it's been trying to heal itself. We'll just give it a bit of a helping hand with a dressing and it'll soon be good as new.'

'Still don't see why I had to take my trousers off. You could have just hiked them up a bit to look at a scratch.'

Nick silently rolled his eyes and Polly had to stifle a chuckle, her fingers working quickly and deftly as she covered the wound to protect it from further knocks while it finished healing.

'You'll need to go to your doctor's surgery to have the dressing changed, Mr Ferguson. . .'

'Haven't got a doctor any more,' he interrupted her. 'He died several years ago, and the new one's too young to know what he's doing.'

Polly didn't dare look at Nick for fear she'd start laughing. Luckily, he took charge of the conversation.

'In which case, you'd better come back here for someone to change the dressing and keep an eye on it.'

'I won't have to take my trousers off again, will I?' he demanded suspiciously, looking from one to the other.

'No. Next time you can tell the nurse that you only need to roll your trouser-leg up,' Nick confirmed.

As Polly escorted the elderly man across to Reception to arrange another appointment she wasn't certain whether it was a good idea—after all, some poor nurse was going to have to work uncomfortably close to those awful trousers. But at least they wouldn't have to fight the elderly man to get him to take them off so perhaps the one outweighed the other.

She turned away from the appointments desk and glanced down at her fob watch, surprised to see that it was only a couple of minutes to the end of her shift.

Suddenly she realised how tired and hungry she felt, and she sighed at the thought of the shopping she would have to do on her way home if she was going to have anything to eat.

She was just passing the emergency reception area when a pair of headlights stabbed through the gloom beyond the automatic doors as an ambulance sped into view and reversed swiftly up to the emergency entrance.

In spite of the fact that it was the end of her shift, there was no way she could ignore the urgency of the vehicle's arrival.

As she began to hurry towards it her instincts told her that something terrible was happening inside, and she was almost running by the time the back doors flew open.

CHAPTER NINE

THE first person to emerge from the back of the ambulance was Ted Larrabee and he didn't bother with the steps to the vehicle, gaining the entrance ramp with a leap which continued into a run straight towards Polly.

For a second Polly's step faltered when she saw the tiny bundle cradled in the paramedic's arms, but her training kicked in instantaneously.

'This way.' She indicated the closest emergency room. 'What's happened?'

'SIDS.' The hated acronym almost disappeared in the sound of the mobile respirator he was squeezing, and Polly was glad she was holding the door for him or the sudden shock would have had her on her knees.

No! Not today! she screamed inside her head. *It's too soon . . .*

Outwardly, apart from the stark whiteness of her knuckles as she clutched the door, she was totally in control, releasing her grip to hurry across as he deposited his tiny burden and restarted heart massage alternately with oxygenation.

'He's four months old and he didn't wake for his feed. Slightly snuffly earlier in the day but otherwise perfectly healthy,' Ted continued, reciting the stark facts.

Without a second's hesitation Polly began to check the child, firing questions about how long it was since the parents had last seen the child and whether resuscitation had been initiated as soon as the ambulance was called.

One part of her mind was registering the facts—that the child had been put down for a sleep and hadn't woken for his next feed; that he was already cold when the horrified mother had discovered what had happened; that the parents had started CPR themselves while they'd waited for the ambulance to arrive, then had followed the vehicle in their own car while the paramedics had taken over the attempt at resuscitation.

The other part of her mind was screaming out in denial at the fact that it had already been too late when the baby had been found.

Somehow it always seemed to be too late, she thought as her heart tore apart inside her.

It wasn't fair!

He was a beautiful, healthy little boy. There was absolutely nothing wrong with him except a touch of the snuffles. She'd been caring for him properly. She was a good mother.

It wasn't right!

He hadn't deserved to die. He'd deserved a long, happy life and she'd loved him so much. . .so very much. . .

'Polly. . .? Sister!'

It wasn't Ted's voice which brought her out of the living nightmare, but Nick's. *His* arm which circled her shaking shoulders and offered her a handful of paper handkerchiefs to mop up the tears which streamed down her cheeks to fall on the pale, still body.

'Ross MacFadden's on his way down, Polly,' he said quietly, using the familiar paediatric consultant's name to help to steady her.

She suddenly realised that Ted had gone and she was

alone in the room with Nick and the tiny still figure on the bed beside them, and she had no recollection of anything that had happened after she'd realised that the little boy was dead and there was nothing she could do about it.

Memory had taken over and she'd been totally immersed in her own personal nightmare.

'Ross will take over here and speak to the parents,' Nick continued, his soothing voice reassuring her by telling her all the things she already knew. 'He'll tell them what's happened and see if they want to spend some time with their little boy to say their goodbyes.'

'But. . .'

Somehow, in spite of the fact that she knew that there was absolutely nothing either of them could do for him, she couldn't bring herself to leave. It didn't seem right that the little boy should be left all alone—as if he'd been abandoned.

'Hannah's waiting to come in and sit with him. We won't leave him by himself,' Nick said, as if he'd understood what she was thinking without her having to say anything.

'Come on, Polly,' he prompted softly when she paused by the door and looked back one last time. 'It's time to go home.'

Polly looked up at him, at the compassion in his eyes, and realised that somehow he knew what she was going through; knew why she had reacted this way to someone else's tragedy, and she knew that she could trust him to take care of her.

'I need to get my things,' she mumbled as her mind began to function again. 'My clothes and my bag from my locker. And my shoes. . . They were wet this morning. . .'

Was it really just this morning that she and Hannah
had sheltered under her umbrella? It seemed as if a
decade had passed and she felt as if she'd aged a
century.

'We'll detour past your locker and then I'm driving
you home,' he said decisively, as he pushed the door
open and nodded to Hannah.

'Oh, but you can't just leave the hospital without. . .'

'Polly, I'm off duty too,' he said, giving her shoulder
a little shake and indicating with his free hand the fact
that he'd already exchanged his white coat for his suit
jacket. 'I was handing over just as the ambulance arrived
so I'm free to play chauffeur.'

'Oh.' She subsided, suddenly conscious that,
although he wasn't tempting the hospital grapevine by
walking along the corridor with his arm still wrapped
around her shoulders, he was still holding her arm.

The warmth of Nick's fingers penetrated the fabric
of her sleeve as he held her, his grasp as gentle as if
he thought she was as fragile as a Dresden figurine.

He waited for her to retrieve her belongings, and
when she rejoined him in the corridor he wove his
fingers between hers and led her out to his car.

Polly sank into the luxurious upholstery and as soon
as she'd fastened the seat belt she closed her eyes
wearily and leant back.

As if in a dream, she listened to Nick sliding into
the car beside her and heard the smooth thrum of the
engine as he turned the key and set off through the
darkness.

Time didn't seem to have any meaning as she sat
trapped in an endless replay of the nightmare scenes in
her mind.

She was vaguely aware that she had started crying

again but it was Nick's gentle ministrations as he used his own handkerchief to dry her tears that finally made her open her eyes, and she realised that the car had stopped.

She drew in a deep shuddering breath and reached for the seat belt release so that she didn't have to meet his eyes.

'Thank you for bringing me home,' she whispered as she reached for her bag, which had slipped off her lap and onto the floor by her feet. 'I—I'll see you tomorrow.'

She went to open the door but paused when she heard Nick's soft chuckle.

'Polly. . .look out of the window.'

Puzzled, she did as he said and felt a slow wash of heat scorch her cheeks when she saw where they were.

'I'm sorry, I didn't realise we'd come to your house. Did. . .? Do you want me to walk the rest of the. . .?'

'Don't be silly,' he chided gently, not waiting for her to finish her question. 'I've brought you here because I don't think you should be on your own just yet. If you'll accept my hospitality I can promise you a reasonably good cup of tea.'

She summoned up a watery smile and nodded, grateful for the fact that she wouldn't be going into an empty flat just yet, then sat limply and watched as he came round to her side of the car to help her out.

'What do you want first—the tea or the bathroom?' he offered when he'd closed the front door behind her and she found herself once more in the welcoming warmth of his hallway.

Suddenly she had a mental image of what she must look like. Her uniform was rumpled after a day's work and she had never managed to look pretty when she

cried so could just imagine how red and blotchy her
eyes were.

'The bathroom, please,' she said wryly, and turned
towards the little ground-floor cloakroom.

'How about a long hot shower and a change of
clothes?' he suggested, one dark blond eyebrow raised
questioningly.

Polly's initial reaction was to refuse the offer, but
the thought of standing under steaming hot water and
washing all the stress and tension down the drain was
too enticing.

'That would be wonderful, but are you sure. . .?'

'I'm sure.' He smiled his approval and gestured for
her to go up. 'Do you remember the way? There are
clean towels on the rail and more in the airing cupboard
if you need them. Take your time.'

She was conscious that he was watching her as she
made her way up the still-uncarpeted stairs, and knew
that he didn't start walking towards the kitchen until she
reached the top and turned towards the bathroom door.

Just that small demonstration of concern was enough
to start her crying again, and she hurried to strip off
her clothes and climb under the pelting spray to disguise
the sounds of her distress.

Polly didn't really know how long it was before she
finally climbed out of the shower, and she felt a twinge
of guilt for the amount of hot water she must have used.
Then she wrapped herself in one of Nick's enormous
towels and realised that she felt too exhausted to care
about anything other than the fact that she wasn't alone.

'Polly?' The deep voice was accompanied by tapping
on the door. 'How are you doing in there? Are you
nearly ready for something to eat?'

Now that she was out of the shower she realised that

the room was full of the tantalising aromas of cooking, drifting up from the kitchen below, and Polly gave a rusty chuckle when her stomach gave a loud rumble of appreciation.

'Suddenly I'm starving and I'm nowhere near ready to come down. My hair's still soaking,' she called.

'Well, why not wrap it in a hand-towel and borrow the robe on the back of the door?' he suggested after a pause, his voice sounding strangely rough. 'It'll be miles too long but you can always roll the sleeves up.'

'Oh, but. . .' Polly began, the very idea of sharing a meal with Nick while dressed in nothing more than his robe sending sharp shivers of awareness up the back of her neck.

'The food will spoil if you leave it until your hair's dry,' he prompted. 'Mushroom omelette and crusty bread rolls,' he added, tempting her beyond bearing.

'All right! All right! I'm coming down!' she surrendered swiftly. 'Don't you start on mine before I get there!'

She felt self-conscious when she padded down in her bare feet, with his towelling robe wrapped nearly twice around her, but when he teasingly hovered his fork over a plump button mushroom on her plate she rushed to protect her food and the discomfort was gone.

When they'd finished eating, Nick insisted that she left the plates stacked on the drainer and carried the tea-tray through to the lounge.

He must have lit the fire while she was under the shower because it was now burning brightly in the refurbished fireplace, adding a cheery warmth to the room.

'I can't remember the last time I sat in front of an open fire,' Polly mused as she gazed vacantly at the patterns made by the flames, her feet tucked up beside her on the settee with the hem of Nick's robe pulled down to enclose them.

'I read somewhere that it's a tribal comfort symbol,' Nick said in a relaxed voice, and she looked across at him to watch the way the flickers of the flames glimmered along the thick blond strands of his hair and gleamed in his half-closed eyes. 'Apparently, it's supposed to be some sort of universal memory from our long-ago cave-dwelling ancestors. . . Just sitting in front of it is supposed to make us feel more secure.'

Silence fell and stretched out as Polly thought about what he'd said, and she found herself agreeing.

'I can see what you mean,' she murmured, looking back at the fire before he caught her gazing at him. 'It's as if you know that the fire can protect you from all the nasty predators, lurking out there in the darkness.'

'And the nightmares?' he suggested softly, and she felt his eyes on her. This time she felt compelled to meet his gaze.

'Maybe,' she conceded equally softly, in spite of the nervous way her pulse had begun to race.

She had known, subconsciously, when she'd accepted his invitation to take her home that they would eventually talk about the cause of her ignominious collapse in the presence of the dead child.

Part of her had been afraid of it—she had been trying to cope with that particular nightmare alone for five years—but now that the time had finally come she felt almost at peace with herself.

Drawing in a deep shuddering breath, she leant back into her corner of the settee and closed her eyes while she searched for the courage to begin.

The sudden warmth of his hand as it covered hers startled her into opening her eyes again, and she turned her head to face him, strengthened by the caring gesture.

'I suppose you've guessed that I lost a baby to SIDS—a little boy almost the same age as that one today,' she began in a husky voice, her eyes stinging with the renewed threat of tears.

He murmured a wordless agreement and the compassion she saw in his eyes helped her to continue.

'I'd just returned to work part time after my maternity leave. Tim didn't want me to. He thought I ought to stay at home full time and devote myself to being a wife and mother. We argued about it, and I said we needed the money—and we did, if we wanted to have a decent holiday and replace the car—but really I wanted to go back because I enjoyed my job.'

She paused, having to fight a little harder for control as she drew closer to the nightmare, until she felt the slight squeeze he gave her fingers. It was all the encouragement she needed to grit her teeth and go on.

'I was lucky to get a place in the crèche provided by the hospital and, apart from the fact that Tim picked a fight every time I was late or the house wasn't tidy, I had started to get into a routine and I thought it was all working out.'

She had to stop to swallow hard, her throat nearly closed by the lump of misery put there by the memories she was dredging up. Then she began again, her words coming faster and faster as she was bombarded by details.

'Andrew had been a bit snuffly the day before, but I thought perhaps he'd picked a bit of a cold up from one of the other children in the crèche. I strapped his carrycot in the safety harness on the back seat of the car to drive him to the hospital, and he was just dozing off to sleep as I set off.

'I had the local radio station on and there was a newsflash about an accident, blocking the road I wanted to take and warning drivers to take an alternative route. It was a bit longer, but at least I wouldn't get stuck in a big snarl-up and be late for work.

'It must have taken me about half an hour altogether, and I was just s-signalling to turn into the hospital car park when I caught sight of Andrew in the mirror and I just *knew* that there was something wrong.'

She was shaking all over, in spite of the fact that somewhere during her recitation Nick had put his arm around her shoulders and pulled her close to his side.

'I. . .I drove straight to the emergency department entrance with my hand on the hooter and. . .and they w-worked on him for half an hour, but it was already too l-late. The coroner said he must have d-died shortly after I set off.'

'Ah, sweetheart, hush,' Nick murmured into the silky strands of her towel-dried hair as she fought for breath.

'He. . . He blamed me,' she said in a voice full of misery. 'Tim said it was *my* fault Andrew died. He said if I'd stayed at home the way he'd wanted I'd have been taking care of him properly instead of taking care of other peoples' children. He said. . .he said. . .'

She couldn't go on, the memory of Tim's rejection and condemnation fuelling her sobs until they obliterated any coherent speech as she wept her heart out on Nick's broad shoulder.

When Polly's grief finally subsided into hiccups and copious nose-blowing she discovered that at some time Nick had pulled her onto his lap and she was totally surrounded by the warmth and security of his arms. Even so, she was embarrassed to have poured everything out like that.

'I'm sorry,' she whispered. 'I've never. . .never made a fool of myself like that before.'

'Then it was time you did,' he said firmly, squashing her attempts at sliding off his knees by the simple expedient of tightening his hold on her. 'Wasn't there anyone you could talk to? Didn't the hospital put you in touch with a counsellor?'

She shook her head. 'They offered, but I couldn't. . . couldn't bear to talk about it.'

'So you locked it all inside.'

His knowing tone drew her eyes up to meet his and the expression there confirmed what she'd suspected.

'You did the same thing,' she said softly. 'Locked all the pain away and cut yourself off.'

She felt his chest expand as he sighed. 'At the time it was the only way I could cope.'

Polly nodded and murmured, almost under her breath, 'If I didn't let anyone get close then it wouldn't hurt when I lost them. . .' Her voice trailed away and as the silence lengthened she became aware of a new tension in the strong arms that surrounded her.

'I. . .I ought to be getting back home,' she said, trying to find some way out of an increasingly awkward situation.

Out of the kindness of his heart Nick had given her a lift home after she'd come apart at the seams. He'd even thrown in a shower and a hot meal, and she'd repaid him by weeping and wailing on his shoulder. He must be heartily sick of the sight of her and wishing her gone by now. It was just politeness which was stopping him from. . .

'You're not going anywhere, Polly. . .except upstairs to bed.'

Shock had her eyes flying up to meet his, the echoes

of his husky words still whirling round inside her head.

'*What. . .!*' she whispered, and felt her eyes widening.

She was incapable of anything else, robbed of breath by the mental images of their night together which had joined the words already short-circuiting her brain. His warmth and strength when he'd held her cradled in his arms; the leashed power in his body as he'd braced himself over her before he'd joined their two bodies, and the expression on his face when ecstasy held him in thrall; his naked body stretched out on his beautiful bed in the abandon of sleep, and her last view of him after they'd spent the night together.

'Polly. . .you'll catch flies,' he teased as he touched her chin with the tip of one finger, and she flushed as she snapped her mouth shut.

'Well, you said. . .you said. . .'

'I said you were going upstairs to bed,' Nick repeated, his voice very serious now. 'You're tired and upset and I don't think you need the hassle of getting dressed to go home, then spending the night alone in your flat.'

He paused and Polly's heart sank at the prosaic reasoning, no matter how caring the sentiments were.

'Of course,' he continued, his voice taking on a slight roughness, 'if you were to tell me that you'd rather not spend the night in my house, or if you were to tell me that you'd rather spend the night in your own bed, I'd willingly take you home.'

'But. . .?' Polly challenged softly, a little frisson of excitement causing her pulse rate to pick up, and she marvelled at the recovery rate of the human body.

'What?'

'I heard a "but" at the end of that sentence,' she said as she gazed at him, and even in the subdued lighting of the room, she saw the betraying hint of colour shade his cheekbones.

'But. . .if you want to stay here. . .with me. . . If. . .' He paused and she felt his chest expand sharply as he drew in a swift breath before he continued speaking; felt the tension in the body which curved protectively around her and the arms which still surrounded her. 'If you want to share my bed so that I can be there for you and take care of you the way you took care of me when I fell apart. . .'

'If?' she repeated, and felt the smile creep over her face. 'I can't think of anything I want more. . .*need* more than to have you hold me and keep the nightmares away.'

The small voice inside her head was screaming out a warning, telling her that she was risking heartbreak and misery if she offered herself so openly, but for the first time in five years she didn't care.

Subconsciously she realised that there had been no mention of love on either side, but suddenly she could see a glimmer of light in the darkness and if there was any chance that it would turn into the warmth of full sun she was willing to take the chance.

Perhaps Nick wouldn't ever be able to let go of his grief over Deanne and their unborn child and perhaps she would never find the courage to have another child but, in the meantime, they could find comfort in each other and, perhaps, in time. . .

It was almost as if Nick had been paralysed by secret voices of his own because it was several seconds before he reacted to her acceptance with a release of the tension which had gripped him in a long exhaled breath.

'I'll keep you safe,' he promised as he slid one arm

under her legs as if he was going to lift her into his arms and carry her upstairs.

'Nick! I can walk!' Polly objected, and wriggled round on his lap to put her feet on the floor. She ignored the involuntary groan he quickly stifled, in spite of the fact that she was only too aware of the reason for his discomfort and inordinately pleased that she'd had such an effect on him.

'In fact,' she continued briskly as she reached for the tea-tray, 'I'm going to take these cups through into the kitchen and do that washing up while you go and have your shower—if there's any hot water left.'

'You don't have to do that,' he objected with a frown as he straightened to his full six feet. 'It's not one of the conditions of you staying here, you know.'

'I know,' she said with an impish grin, then lowered her voice to continue. 'But you did promise to take care of me the way I took care of you last time and, if my memory serves me right, you started off with a shower that time.'

She turned away and walked out of the room, almost laughing aloud at the stunned expression in his eyes.

As she began to deal with the few items they'd used she was conscious of several minutes' silence before Nick's footsteps sounded in the hallway.

She heard him turn the key in the front door to lock the rest of the world out, then followed his hollow tread on the bare wood as he went up the stairs. As she squeezed washing-up liquid into the water she wondered what he had been thinking about as he'd stood in the sitting-room so silently.

Then she heard the sound of the shower running in the bathroom up above and her imagination ran riot. She visualised the way his body would gleam as the water poured over each curve and hollow and the way his hands would spread the soap over his chest, rubbing it into the curly hair which spread across the width of his chest and down towards. . .

Stop it! she ordered herself as she nearly dropped the plate she'd been polishing for what seemed like the last week. Get the job finished and then you can go upstairs and see for yourself, if that's what he wants you to do.

There was no doubt in her mind that he wanted her in his bed—the powerful reaction of his body when he'd cradled her on his lap told her that. But she knew that Nick was an honourable man, and if he had decided that all he was going to do was hold her in his arms to keep the nightmares away. . .

She chuckled silently at the irony of the situation.

Here she was, a divorcee of five years who had decided unequivocally that she was never going to allow another man to get close enough to hurt her, and what was she contemplating? Only the best way to persuade the man she'd fallen in love with to take her into his bed and make love to her until he fell as deeply in love with her as she was with him. . . Only the best way to show him exactly how much he meant to her and how much she wanted to spend the rest of her life with him.

Not much. . .really!

Polly reached out one shaking hand to turn off the light and padded her way almost silently along the hall. She realised how nervous she was when she tried to climb the stairs and her knees refused to comply.

'Idiot!' she muttered under her breath as she grabbed hold of the bannister rail and heaved herself upwards, nearly tripping over the hem of his voluminous robe.

'You can't show him anything if you're down here and he's up there!'

She reached the top of the stairs and hovered uncertainly, not knowing where Nick was. Had he already gone into the bedroom? Was he sitting up and waiting for her to join him in the polished wooden splendour of his bed?

For just one second she contemplated racing back down the stairs and curling up in front of the fire for the night, but then the bathroom door opened and Nick came out, wearing nothing but a towel wrapped round his hips, and she was lost.

For timeless moments her besotted eyes roamed greedily over him, charting the actuality of the memories which had been tormenting her, and he looked even better than she remembered—taller, broader, more perfectly symmetrical, more virile and infinitely more. . .

'Polly,' he whispered huskily, interrupting the increasingly lascivious train of her thoughts, 'if you keep looking at me like that we're not only going to set the towel alight but probably the whole house!'

'Nick!' She covered her flaming cheeks with her hands, horrified that he'd seen her ogling him like that and tempted once again to flee.

'Come here, sweetheart,' he ordered softly and spread his arms wide in invitation. 'Come to me, Polly.' And his eyes gleamed like softly polished silver in the half-light as she flew into them.

CHAPTER TEN

NICK came awake slowly, surprised to find that the bedside light was still on. He usually turned it off before he lay in the darkness, trying to ignore his demons long enough to snatch a few hours of fitful sleep.

He turned his head to look at the clock on the bedside cabinet to see how many hours he'd managed this time, and suddenly realised that he wasn't alone in the bed. There was a tousled dark head sharing the pillow with him.

Moving carefully so that he didn't disturb her, he rolled over and propped himself up on one elbow, then he allowed himself the luxury of gazing down at her.

'*Polly*,' he whispered soundlessly, just for the pleasure of using her name as he charted the perfection of her features relaxed in sleep.

Not that either of them had had much time for sleep, he thought ruefully as he remembered their hunger for each other. He snorted softly as his body stirred again. How could he have thought he had sated himself with her last night when, just hours later, he needed to bury himself in her again so badly that he could hardly wait for her to wake?

Was it just lust? The overwhelming result of his self-enforced celibacy?

He shook his head.

No. This feeling didn't have anything to do with rampant hormones—well, maybe a little, he admitted as his lower anatomy reacted to his perusal of the pink-tipped perfection of her breast, peeping over the edge of the bedclothes.

This was *more* than just hormones, he corrected himself as he contemplated the new peace which filled his hungry soul.

He'd been in love before, and if Deanne had lived he would probably still be happy with her and the child they'd made between them. But she was gone and, whether he wanted it to or not, life had moved on.

He drew in a shaky breath as he felt the tight bands loosen around his heart.

The word 'love' seemed too small to encompass the enormity of the emotion he felt as he realised that it was Polly who had filled the empty spaces inside him, Polly who had taken him by the scruff of the neck and made him face his shortcomings, Polly who had understood the pain and the guilt and whose resilience in the face of her own tragedy had finally taught him to look towards the future.

He couldn't resist the temptation to look at her again and carefully lifted the edge of the bedclothes away from her body so that the soft light could touch her, spilling over the pale curves and hollows as if she were a statue in palest pink living marble.

The cooler air reached her breasts and he watched with pleasure as her nipples tightened in reaction, the flesh darkening into tempting berries that he longed to take into his mouth.

Greatly daring, he pursed his lips and blew a soft stream of air towards them and was rewarded when not only did they grow more prominent, more enticing, but Polly shifted in her sleep, arching her back as though offering her breasts for him to taste.

Nick licked his lips in anticipation and smiled lazily.

Polly didn't have to go to the hospital until later today and he'd been accustomed to functioning on too little sleep for years so what difference would it make if he lost a little more because he'd seduced Polly into waking up for another session of the most mind-blowing love-making he'd ever known?

He licked the tip of one finger and was just reaching out to dampen one tightly furled rosy bud when the realisation hit him full force and he froze.

That was the difference. That was what made everything different with Polly. The word 'love-making' said it all.

Nick drew in a deep breath as certainty poured through him and he smiled again.

He loved her, right to the depths of his soul, and as soon as she was awake he would tell her so and ask her to marry him.

His smile dimmed slightly when he remembered the way she had sobbed her heart out in his arms when she'd told him about the loss of her child. He had felt a measure of that same grief and could well understand why she had cut herself off from any further hurt.

Last night had changed all that.

Last night she had been ready to consciously and willingly share his bed, and that meant that she must love him, too.

As he gazed down at her a flood of certainty overtook him as he looked towards a future filled with the presence of Polly and the children they would one day create.

He had a sudden image of a tiny mouth, greedily suckling at her, and desire to do the same twisted deep inside him.

He licked his finger again and reached out towards the tip of her breast, circling her nipple with moisture before he blew on it very softly.

As he'd hoped, the cool breeze caused the delicate flesh to darken and tighten still further and Polly stirred again, the pattern of her breathing changing with her unconscious excitement. This time she shifted her legs restlessly, tilting her hips so that her thighs parted—as if in anticipation of the pleasures he wanted to give her.

He'd been amazed how sensitive her breasts had been when he'd stroked and suckled them last night—so sensitive that, as he was doing now, he could bring her to full arousal without touching the rest of her body at all.

He settled his head more comfortably on his hand, and prepared to be as patient and as thorough as he knew how. He would enjoy seeing if he could bring her the same pleasure while she was still asleep—he couldn't imagine a more erotic way of waking her up to ask her to marry him. . .

'Damn!' His hand froze again when he heard a distant sound and realised that it was his pager. He must have left it in the bathroom when he'd had his shower last night—the first time he'd ever forgotten to bring it into the bedroom with him.

But, then, he *had* been rather distracted last night, wondering if he was going to lie in agony all night while Polly slept in his arms—or whether he really had seen the gleam in her eyes which meant that she was looking forward to sharing a bed with him as much as he was with her.

With a last regretful look at the ripe perfection of her engorged breasts he softly lowered the bedclothes over them and slid out of bed to pad, naked, towards the bathroom. If he didn't get to that pager soon and turn it off it might wake Polly, and he wanted that pleasure for himself.

He was smiling as he passed the mirror in the bathroom and saw the wolfish glint in his eyes when he remembered just how little sleep he'd allowed her to have before exhaustion had claimed them both, then he swatted the infernal gadget to silence the noise.

Five minutes later he was glumly padding back up the stairs to retrieve his clothes.

John Preece had taken over from him at the end of his shift, and Nick had noticed that he didn't look quite up to par. Since then he'd gone down with a monumental migraine and wasn't fit to work so, in line with the rota drawn up for A and E cover, Nick was going to have to turn out to take John's place.

He held his breath as the wardrobe door creaked when he opened it, then reached inside for a clean shirt and looped a tie around his neck. His shoes were in the bathroom and his keys. . .

He paused in the doorway for one last look.

God! She looked so beautiful lying there, her dark hair and dark lashes such a stunning contrast to her pale skin and her lips still slightly swollen and rosy after the tumultuous kisses they'd shared.

He glanced at the clock, wondering what the chances were that she'd still be asleep when he returned. If she was then perhaps he could still enact his fantasy of arousing her to wakefulness and a heartfelt proposal of marriage.

He shook his head.

No chance of that now, and he didn't want to break her sleep just to tell her that he'd been called in to the hospital. He'd have to write a note to make certain that she knew that he'd be thinking of her. . .

Polly stretched as she woke and winced at the unaccustomed ache in muscles she'd all but forgotten she had, then smiled like the cat that had got the cream when she remembered what she'd done to make them ache like that.

'Mmm. . . Nick?' she murmured, feeling too lazy even to open her eyes, and reached out a hand to stroke him—but he wasn't there.

She surged up from the covers, her eyes wide open now as she gazed anxiously around the room. There wasn't a sound to be heard—nothing from the bathroom and nothing from the ground floor of the house to tell her where he was.

She sat there for a moment, listening and shivering slightly as the air touched the warmth of her naked back, and she knew that the house was empty.

It didn't take her long to decide that she was just wasting her time, sitting there, and she slid to the edge of the bed before dashing, barefoot and stark naked, across the partially renovated hallway and into the bathroom.

Wherever Nick was she would probably have to wait until she got to the hospital to find out what had. . .

Glancing towards the mirror over the sink to see what sort of tangled mess the night had made of her hair, she was startled into laughter.

All over the mirror, written in soap, was a message from Nick.

'Called in. John sick. See you soon. Don't use all the hot water!'

There was a smear at the bottom which could have

been more writing, or his name, but she couldn't read it.

She laughed again as she stepped into the shower, hugging the thought to herself that he'd cared enough about her to leave a message to tell her why he'd had to leave.

As she turned her face up to the spray she couldn't help the smile which grew at the thought that perhaps he was closer to loving her than she'd realised. He'd certainly been very loving when she'd bared her soul last night and told him about Andrew and then, when he'd taken her to his bed. . .

She reached for the soap and began to spread the lather over her shoulders, remembering the way he had pushed his robe off them and kissed his way down her neck and then further down over the slopes of her breasts. . .

As she remembered the way he'd explored her curves her hands were retracing his path until she was cupping them in her palms. She marvelled at the way they felt so heavy, so sensitive, when all she was doing was remembering the way he'd taken them in his much larger hands and finessed her nipples until she'd been moaning with desire.

Even now they were so engorged that it was almost painful to touch them, and she wondered for a moment if it was a result of his attention to them.

She remembered the obvious pleasure he'd taken in finding out what pleased her most, and the delight he'd taken in suckling her until she couldn't bear the suspense any longer and had taken matters into her own hands.

As she stood under the spray to rinse the lather away she marvelled at the fact that just the play of the water droplets over her breasts made the tingling spread deep down inside her as her body prepared itself for him.

She didn't think her body had ever been this responsive before. The last time she'd felt anything like it was when she was. . .was when she was pregnant. . .

The shocking thought came to her so suddenly that her knees refused to bear her weight and she nearly collapsed in a heap, just barely managing to hang onto the tap while she turned the water off and staggered out onto the mat.

Pregnant?

Polly shivered convulsively and reached for a towel to wrap it tightly around herself.

She couldn't be pregnant. It was impossible. She didn't want to be pregnant ever again. . . She couldn't stand the anguish of waiting for something terrible to happen to her baby. She'd only just survived the loss of Andrew. She couldn't—wouldn't—put herself through that again. She was too frightened.

In spite of the fact that she'd just climbed out of a hot shower, she was icy cold through and through. As she mentally added up the days which had passed since the first time they'd made love the weight of dread wiped her silly smile away. How could she not have realised sooner?

Even when Nick had taken pains to protect her last night she hadn't remembered that their first time together had been too explosive for either of them to think of their responsibilities.

And it wasn't just herself she had to think of—there was Nick, too.

She'd known right from the first that he was still in love with his wife, and the guilt that he was still alive had stopped him from even contemplating a commitment to anyone else.

They'd each known the pain of losing a child and, while she knew how well he related to their smaller patients in the department, he'd never said anything about wanting a family—and she could hardly expect him to change his life just because she was expecting a baby.

Yet even if she were willing to have the child without his support—without anyone's support—there was no way that she would be able to cope alone. . .

Polly drew in a shuddering breath, conscious that her thoughts were chasing each other round and round. At the moment she was too shocked at the mere idea that she was pregnant to be able to think clearly.

The only logical idea in her head was that she had to get dressed and go back to her flat to change. Then, on the way to work, she would make a detour into the local chemist for a kit to test herself.

When she had the result she would know that it was time to start making decisions.

Positive.

It felt as if the word must be engraved across her forehead she kept thinking about it so often.

When she'd done the test she'd fixed her eyes on the sweep hand of her watch while she waited for the chemical reaction to take place. Right up to the second she looked up from her watch and focused on the tell-tale colour change she had hoped that she was wrong, but she wasn't that lucky.

Now she just had to try to keep her mind on her job until the end of her shift. Then she would have to decide what she was going to do and when she was going to do it.

Her mind shied away from the narrow range of

options open to her, and she concentrated on taping a young man's fingers together to support the one he'd injured.

'How did you say you cracked the bone?' she asked, longing to hear anything but the sound of her own thoughts.

'I. . .er. . .I had an argument with a door,' he said sheepishly.

'You argued with a door?' Polly knew from his expression that there was more to the story and she flicked him a grin. 'And the door won?'

'Well, it was locked.'

'Wouldn't a key have helped?' she suggested, surprised to feel a bubble of laughter rising at the mental image. It was a relief to find out that her sense of the ridiculous was still intact, in spite of the problems weighing her down.

'Yeah, except my girlfriend had the key and she was on the other side of the door—just because I stayed late at my mate's and forgot to pick her up from work!'

'And it always looks so easy on the television when the hero smacks the door and it just bursts open, doesn't it? You never see them going round with a broken finger in the next scene.'

'No. And if my girlfriend sees these little bits of tape around my fingers she's not going to believe that I broke it either. Couldn't you put something. . . bigger. . .on it?'

'Ah.' Polly nodded her understanding. 'Trying for the sympathy vote? Will it help if I tell you that you'll need to rest it in a sling for the first day or two?'

'Really?' The young man's eyes brightened. 'And if I get some cotton wool for padding—just so it doesn't get knocked or anything.'

'And if you take her some flowers to apologise for losing your temper and some chocolates to apologise for forgetting to pick her up?' Polly suggested. 'And while you're playing the wounded soldier don't forget to move your fingers every so often to keep the circulation going. You want the finger to mend while you're getting all that sympathy.'

She was still smiling when he disappeared in the direction of the reception area, but the sound of Nick's voice in a nearby room soon wiped it off her face.

As she hurried towards the next waiting patient she thought wryly that it was all too easy to give advice to others but it was far harder to organise her own life.

Ever since she'd come on duty she'd been avoiding Nick, knowing that she daren't risk talking to him until she'd had time to think. But that didn't mean that she hadn't found herself watching him when he was working nearby, her eyes searching out his mannerisms for her heart to store away.

She knew that he'd been watching her too. She had felt his eyes like a caress as she'd gone about her own work and, in spite of the fact that he was operating on less sleep than usual, there was a noticeable spring to his step and a hint of a smile in his eyes.

Thank goodness he would be going off duty soon. At least she could relax for the second half of her shift without worrying about staying out of his way. Somehow today it seemed that every time she turned around he was there. . .

'Sister Lang?'

As if her thoughts had conjured him up out of thin air, he was right behind her.

'Yes, Doctor?' she replied formally, ever conscious that any number of people could eavesdrop on their conversation. All it would take was a hint of intimacy between them and the hospital grapevine would blow it out of all proportion in no time.

'Any chance of having a word with you when you go for your break?' he asked, and Polly was powerless to stop her pulse responding to his ruffled hair and the sleepy, sexy look in his eyes. But she had to start pulling away—had to learn how to resist the attraction before it destroyed her.

'I'm sorry, but I've already had my break,' she lied, squashing the impulse to cross her fingers while her heart continued to beat a rapid tattoo. 'Was it anything important?'

He was silent for a moment, a frown pleating his forehead as his silvery eyes searched her face. He had obviously recognised the new coolness in her tone and he was already trying to analyse the reason.

'It can wait till later,' he conceded. 'I'm off home now to catch up on some sleep.'

Polly must have said something before she turned away but all she could think was that she would have loved to share a secret smile with him when he'd mentioned needing sleep; would have loved to see the gleam in his eyes which meant that he, too, was remembering the reason *why* he'd missed so much sleep last night.

As it was, all she could allow herself to feel as she heard his footsteps receding along the corridor was relief that he was leaving her in peace for a while.

Peace? With the decisions she would have to make in the next few days and weeks? She didn't know whether to laugh or cry, and felt horribly close to both.

*   *   *

Polly stepped out into the chilly night and shivered as she drew in a lungful of fresh air while she wrapped her thick padded jacket around her.

'Polly?'

The deep voice reached her before she saw him, waiting by his car.

'Get in. The car's warm.'

Her heart sank.

She wasn't ready to speak to him yet. She hadn't had time to make any of the decisions that needed to be made. She'd barely come to terms with the fact that the test had been positive, and with the majority of the accident and emergency staff in an uproar of anticipation over the imminent Autumn Ball it felt as though her thoughts had been through a mincer.

'Come on. You're getting cold.'

Her feet started to take her towards him while her heart wished that she didn't have to see him again; didn't have to have the conversation which was going to rob her of his friendship, and so much more, and leave her nursing a broken heart.

'I've cooked us a meal,' he announced as she fastened her seat belt and she had to blink back tears.

Don't be so nice to me, the little voice pleaded inside her head. It will make it so much harder to lose you.

The journey was over too soon, and in no time he was ushering her inside the familiar hallway and taking her jacket.

'Right,' he began purposefully as he showed her into the sitting-room, his voice so calm that it raised all the hairs on the back of her neck. 'The casserole is in the oven and won't hurt if it isn't eaten straight away so it's your choice—do you want to eat first or do you want to tell me what the hell's going on?'

Polly took a reflexive step backwards when she finally caught sight of the anger in his face. She hadn't seen his eyes looking that cold and wintry for a long time, and hated the fact that she had put the expression there again.

'I. . .' She gestured helplessly, not knowing what to say. She would rather put this discussion off for ever, but if she suggested eating first she knew she wouldn't be able to swallow a mouthful.

'For God's sake, what's the matter with you?' he stormed. 'Yesterday you were understandably upset but I thought, after last night, that at least you knew you could talk to me. Am I wrong?'

It was the hurt she saw in his eyes that put the first crack in the wall she was hiding behind.

'No, Nick. It's not you, it's me. I. . . I've made a mess of everything and I don't know how. . .' She shook her head.

'Do you regret it. . .going to bed with me?' he demanded in a raw voice. 'Is that why you've been avoiding me all day?'

'No! Oh, Nick, how could I regret it? It was the most. . .most wonderful. . .' Her throat closed completely.

'Then why?' he exploded. 'What's gone wrong between last night and this morning? What did I do? What did I say? Please, Polly, tell me. Don't you know how much I lo—'

'I'm pregnant,' she blurted out baldly, then covered her mouth with both hands as if she wished the words had never escaped.

There was a profound silence in the room and she couldn't bear it.

'It happened that first time,' she explained, driven to

fill the void with sound. 'The time I stayed with you and fell asleep. And then we woke up and I forgot that I wasn't protected, but I didn't even think about it until this morning in the shower when my breasts were tender and then I realised that I'd missed my period and. . . and. . .'

She ran out of words and drew in a shuddering breath, waiting for him to speak but too afraid to look at him.

'Did you hear what I said?' he murmured softly, and she heard the soft tread of his feet as he came towards her.

What *had* he said? She'd been so busy trying to find the words to explain. . .

The touch of his hand on her cheek was the shock which drew her eyes up to meet his, and this time they gleamed gently at her like polished silver.

'I said I love you, Polly Lang, and if John Preece hadn't had the appallingly bad timing to go sick in the middle of his shift I had every intention of asking you to marry me this morning.'

Now Polly knew what it was like to travel from hell to heaven and back again in the space of a few minutes, and the tears slipped silently down her cheeks as she shook her head convulsively.

'I can't,' she cried, feeling as if her heart were being torn out by the roots. 'Didn't you hear what *I* said? I'm pregnant.'

'So we'll have a "slightly premature" baby,' Nick said airily, a smile beginning to curl the corners of his mouth. 'We won't be the first—or the last.'

'But I *can't* have the baby,' she sobbed. 'I couldn't bear it. What would happen if it died too?'

'Oh, sweetheart, don't,' he murmured as he wrapped both arms around her and cradled her head on his shoulder with one comforting palm. 'It doesn't have to be like that. The chances are that this baby will only have to worry about being murdered when it becomes a teenager and drives us insane. Anyway, if you were worried we could always get a monitor. . .'

'*If?*' she howled, and tried to fight her way out of his embrace. '*If* I'm worried? You don't know how many nights I've cried for Andrew, how many days I've sat and wondered what he would have been doing by now if he'd lived.'

'Yes, I have,' he reminded her quietly, and the very softness of his voice acted as a rebuke. 'I've gone through exactly the same thing, wondering about my own child—whether it was a girl or a boy, whether it took after me or Deanne. *You* actually got to welcome Andrew into the world and to hold him. You had time with him to build some memories. . .'

'But. . .' The tears were falling faster as Polly heard the sadness in his voice and saw it in his eyes. Surely he could understand that she daren't risk it again.

'Don't you see, Polly?' He held her shoulders and caught her gaze with his. 'There aren't any guarantees in this life. Some of us lose a wife and child, some of us lose a child and some of us get to keep it all—and there's no way of knowing which it's going to be.'

'But I don't think I could face it again,' she wailed, wishing there was an easy answer.

'*You* won't have to. *We* will—together.'

'But. . .'

'*I'm not Tim.*' This time there was steel in his voice to match the glitter in his eyes, and Polly realised that below his calm exterior was a seething cauldron of emotions.

She went to speak again but he covered her lips with

his fingers and wrapped his other arm tightly around her so that she was held closely against him, breast to chest and thigh to thigh, as he gazed intently into her eyes.

'I know we've never discussed it, and I know we're both carrying too many bad memories around with us, but you have to believe that I would never blame you if this baby suffered the same fate as Andrew. Surely you *know* that I would always stand by you?'

'Yes, of course,' she answered without hesitation. 'But, Nick. . .'

'Hush,' he soothed as he cradled her cheeks in his palms and stroked his thumbs tenderly over her cheekbones. 'First things first. Do you love me?' he demanded huskily, and in spite of all her fears there was only one answer.

'Yes. Oh, yes, Nick, I love you so much,' she replied, and his fingertips moved against her lips like a caress.

'And will you marry me and let me share all your worries and happiness?'

Suddenly she realised that it *was* that simple.

'Oh, Nick. . . You're right,' she whispered happily as she gazed up at him. 'It *is* a case of first things first, and the most important thing is that we love each other. Everything else comes second and we'll take it as it comes. . .together.'

'Was that a yes?' he demanded huskily, his mouth hovering close to hers as he slid his fingers through the silky strands of her tousled dark hair to cradle her head possessively in his palms.

'Oh, yes, Nick, I'll marry you. I love you too much to do anything else.'

*   *   *

'Nick?' Polly murmured as she caught him signalling to Leo across the room. 'What are you doing?'

The Autumn Ball was in full swing and while he would rather have stayed at home with Polly she had pointed out that, as one of the consultants, he was duty bound to make an appearance.

The week since Nick had proposed had passed in a flash, and there had been so much to do that she'd all but forgotten about the hospital fund-raiser until Hannah had reminded her this morning.

'Leo's in fine form,' Nick commented without answering Polly's question. 'I never realised that he was hiding a talent as an auctioneer.'

'He's certainly managing to raise a lot of money for the scanner,' she agreed as she looked around at the shimmering array of evening dresses, complemented beautifully by the stark black and white worn by the majority of the men.

Her own dress was in rich burgundy velvet, which showed her pale skin and dark hair off to perfection, and she was certain that no one in the room wore their formal evening dress as well as Nick did.

The auction was turning out to be a rousing success, the mixture of serious, big-money offerings cleverly balanced by the more light-hearted contributions, with much teasing and laughter to leaven the proceedings.

'The trouble is that the bidding goes so fast on some items that I don't have time to see who's after what. Where has he got to now?'

She ran one carefully painted nail down the list of prizes on offer and had just reached the line detailing the holiday cottage in Brittany when she heard Leo's voice rise to signal another successful conclusion.

'Sold. To Dr Prince,' he announced gleefully. 'And,

although it's not a castle, I hope you have a wonderful honey- , er, holiday!'

Polly gasped. 'Nick! Did you really bid for the week in Brittany?'

'And got it, my love!' he gloated, then bent closer to murmur in her ear, 'Leo only just stopped himself spilling the beans just then, but how *do* you fancy going there for our honeymoon?'

'Oh, could we?' Polly knew that her eyes were shining with pleasure as she gazed up at Nick.

To avoid any hullabaloo, they'd tried to keep the fact of their impending marriage very quiet, but suddenly she didn't care *who* saw that she was in love. The hospital grapevine would find out soon enough that they were getting married.

'We can leave right after the ceremony tomorrow,' he said, his eyes full of fervent promises.

Polly thought about the simple ivory-coloured suit hanging ready in the wardrobe next to his deep charcoal one, and smiled.

Neither of them had wanted any ostentation—it would be enough for them to satisfy the legal requirements by exchanging their vows in front of Leo and Hannah. As far as the two of them were concerned, they had already made their committment to each other.

'But what about work?' Her sense of responsibility reared its head at the last minute.

'It's all arranged,' he soothed. 'That new nurse, Hannah's friend, started today.'

'Laura,' Polly supplied.

'That's the one. And I've been in contact with the man who was supposed to join us in a couple of weeks. He's one of Leo's contemporaries—another one I had a hand in training at my last hospital—and I asked him if he could start this week so we could get away.'

Just then Leo began his wind-up for the next item on the agenda, and there was a sudden buzz of interest.

'Now we come to one of tonight's star prizes so will all you lovely ladies take out your tickets and keep an eye on the number because *this* is what you could be winning!'

The lights in the room dimmed and a spotlight lit up the stage area as a man stepped into view. He, too, was dressed in an impeccable evening suit, but his hair was just a little too long and the narrow black domino mask which hid part of his face lent him an air of danger.

Even so, he was the epitome of tall, dark and handsome as he stood there with his shoulders proudly squared and his fists braced on his hips.

'Can we go home now?' Polly prompted as she turned away from the man being greeted by the female contingent with a chorus of wolf whistles.

'Don't you want to wait for the draw?' Nick teased. 'You might be lucky enough to win.'

'I'm not interested,' Polly declared confidently. 'You've helped me to get my priorities in order and I'm a firm believer in first things first.' She looked up at him, knowing that her love was shining in her eyes. 'I've got the man I love and that's enough for me.'

Look next month for Laura's story as she
encounters the charming Wolff Bergen in
SECOND CHANCE

MISSING LINKS

How would you like to win a year's supply of Mills & Boon® books? Well you can and they're FREE! Simply complete the competition below and send it to us by 30th April 1998. The first five correct entries picked after the closing date will each win a year's subscription to the Mills & Boon series of their choice. What could be easier?

1. APPLE   P I E   CRUST

2. STRAWBERRY _ _ _   TARTS

3. MINCED   _ _ _ _   BALLS

4. PICKLED   _ _ _ _ _   RING

5. GRAPE   _ _ _ _ _   JUICE

6. FRENCH   _ _ _ _ _   SAUCE

7. TOFFEE   _ _ _ _ _   CRUMBLE

8. PEANUT   _ _ _ _ _ _ BEANS

9. TANDOORI   _ _ _ _ _ _ _ CURRY

10. PRAWN   _ _ _ _ _ _ _ _ SAUSAGES

Please turn over for details of how to enter ⇨ C7J

HOW TO ENTER

There are ten missing words in our list overleaf. Each of the missing words must link up with the two words on either side to make a type of food.

For example, the word *Pie* links with *Apple* and *Crust* to form *Apple Pie* and *Pie Crust*:

APPLE - PIE - CRUST

As you find each one, write it in the space provided, we've done the first one for you! When you have linked up all the words, don't forget to fill in the coupon below, pop this page in an envelope and post it today—you don't even need a stamp!

Hurry, competition ends 30th April 1998.

Mills & Boon® Missing Links Competition
FREEPOST, Croydon, Surrey, CR9 3WZ

EIRE readers send competition to PO Box 4546, Dublin 24.

Please tick the series you would like to receive
if you are a winner:

Presents™ ❏ Enchanted™ ❏ Medical Romance™ ❏
Historical Romance™ ❏ Temptation® ❏

Are you a Reader Service™ Subscriber?   Yes ❏   No ❏

Ms/Mrs/Miss/Mr _____

(BLOCK CAPS PLEASE)

Address_____

_____

_____ Postcode_____

(I am over 18 years of age)   C7J

One application per household. Competition open to residents of the UK and Ireland only. You may be mailed with offers from other reputable companies as a result of this application. If you would prefer not to receive such offers, please tick box. ❏

Mills & Boon is a registered trademark of
Harlequin Mills & Boon Limited.

MILLS & BOON®

Medical Romance™

COMING NEXT MONTH

WAIT AND SEE by Sharon Kendrick

Despite getting off to a bad start it wasn't long before Maisy and Matthew were appreciating each others professional and personal qualities! But he had issues to resolve before he could offer her a future with him...

TOO CLOSE FOR COMFORT by Jessica Matthews
Sisters at Heart

Adam can't believe it when he reads Naomi's letter of resignation, *"Please understand my reasons and never forget the wonderful time we had together."* What can he do to make her stay?

SECOND CHANCE by Josie Metcalfe
St Augustine's

When Laura wins a dance with a mysterious stranger at the hospital's Autumn Ball, she can't forget it or his kiss. Wolff was appalled, he'd only done it on the understanding that he wouldn't be recognised—but Laura did...

DOCTOR DELICIOUS by Flora Sinclair

Shy, retiring Beth makes a vow, "To stand up for herself!" She transforms herself and Dominic is shocked into treating her as the sophisticated woman she has become. Who does he really love—the old Beth, or the new?

Get swept away by

RISING
Tides

by award-winning author EMILIE RICHARDS

**The reading of a woman's will threatens
to destroy her family.**

*In this explosive sequel to the critically acclaimed
Iron Lace, family, friends and strangers gather for
the reading of Aurore Gerritsen's will. The threat of
an approaching hurricane becomes a minor incident
as each bequest reveals yet another dark family secret.*

Valid only in the UK & Ireland against purchases made in retail outlets
and not in conjunction with any Reader Service or other offer.

50ᵖ OFF
COUPON
VALID UNTIL: 31.1.1998
EMILIE RICHARDS' *RISING TIDES*

To the Customer: This coupon can be used in part payment for a
copy of Emilie Richards' RISING TIDES. Only one coupon can be used
against each copy purchased. Valid only in the UK & Ireland against
purchases made in retail outlets and not in conjunction with any
Reader Service or other offer. Please do not attempt to redeem this
coupon against any other product as refusal to accept may cause
embarrassment and delay at the checkout.

To the Retailer: Harlequin Mills & Boon will redeem this coupon at
face value provided only that it has been taken in part payment for a
copy of Emilie Richards' RISING TIDES. The company reserves the
right to refuse payment against misredeemed coupons. Please submit
coupons to: Harlequin Mills & Boon Ltd. NCH Dept 730, Corby,
Northants NN17 INN.

9 904170 190503 >

0472 00172